THE FAMOUS FIVE AND THE BLUE BEAR MYSTERY

THE FAMOUS FIVE are Julian, Dick George (Georgina by rights), Anne and Timmy the dog.

Back at Kirrin for Christmas, the Five find some very strange things are happening in the town. First someone steals Dr Thompson's Christmas tree, and then there is a peculiar theft at the Kirrin Stores. After a strange lady offers to buy Anne's teddy bear, the Five decide to investigate.

Cover illustration by John Cooper

The Famous Five and the Blue Bear Mystery

A new adventure of the
characters created by
Enid Blyton, told by Claude
Voilier, translated by
Anthea Bell

Illustrated by John Cooper

KNIGHT BOOKS
Hodder and Stoughton

Copyright © Librairie Hachette 1977
First published in France as *Les Cinq vendent la Peau de l'Ours*
English language translation copyright © Hodder & Stoughton
Ltd 1983
Illustrations copyright © Hodder & Stoughton Ltd 1983

First published in Great Britain by Knight Books 1983

British Library C.I.P.

Voilier, Claude
   The Famous Five and the blue bear mystery.
   I. Title   II. Les Cinq vendent la peau de l'ours. *English*
   843'.914[J]   PZ7

ISBN 0-340-32814-2

Printed and bound in Great Britain for
Hodder and Stoughton Paperbacks, a
division of Hodder and Stoughton Ltd.,
Mill Road, Dunton Green, Sevenoaks,
Kent (Editorial Office: 47 Bedford
Square, London, WC1 3DP) by
Hunt Barnard Printing Ltd,
Aylesbury, Bucks.

CONTENTS

1	*Christmas Decorations*	7
2	*The Missing Christmas Tree*	18
3	*The Reporter*	25
4	*The Secret of the Blue Bear*	34
5	*Another Theft*	43
6	*The Motor-Cyclist*	50
7	*An Expedition to Middleton*	60
8	*An Interesting Conversation*	70
9	*The Pink House*	81
10	*In the Cellar*	91
11	*Timmy to the Rescue!*	100
12	*At the Police Station*	110
13	*Back to Kirrin*	119
14	*A Chase at Sea!*	126

Chapter One

CHRISTMAS DECORATIONS

George Kirrin was riding her bicycle along the road to Kirrin village, with her cousins Julian, Dick and Anne. There was a real nip in the air today, which was not so very surprising on December 23rd – but George's blue eyes were shining. She liked the cold, bright weather! And so did the other children. They were all singing at the tops of their voices.

'Good King Wenceslas looked out,
On the feast of Stephen!'

George's dog Timmy, running along beside them and trying to get his paws warm, was the only one of the Five who wasn't so happy. His ears flapped about in the wind, and unlike the children he didn't wear a woolly cap to keep his head warm. But he wouldn't have been separated from his little mistress for anything, so he joined in the carol too, just to show willing, barking loudly as the children sang.

'When the snow lay round about . . . '

'Woof! Woof!'

'Deep and crisp and even!'

Not that there was any snow yet. 'But you never know your luck,' said Julian, who was thirteen and the eldest of the cousins. 'Wouldn't it be fun if we had a white Christmas?'

They cycled round the last bend in the road, and saw the tower of Kirrin church ahead. 'Here we are!' cried George cheerfully. 'Kirrin village – all change! End of the line!'

In fact the children didn't get off their bicycles until they were outside the Kirrin Stores, one of the biggest shops in the village. It sold all sorts of different things, and its window was full of a display of toys and presents – after all, this *was* the day before Christmas Eve!

Julian, Dick and Anne had come to spend the Christmas holidays with George and her parents. Uncle Quentin and Aunt Fanny lived in Kirrin Cottage, a little way from the village itself. It wasn't really a cottage, but quite a big house, and it was about three hundred years old. That morning, Aunt Fanny had asked the children to go and do some shopping for her in the village, because she had found that she was running short of several things, including decorations for the

Christmas tree.

'Oh, look!' cried Anne, the youngest of the four cousins, shaking back her fair hair as she glued her nose to the shop window. 'Isn't it lovely? See those big dolls – and the dear little dolls' teasets, and that electric train with the engine that really whistles, and – '

George and Dick put their heads together too, to admire the window display. They were both dark-haired – and as George, whose real name was Georgina, kept her curly hair short so as to look more like a boy, they might almost have been twin brothers!

'Yes, they've got some super things in there!' agreed Dick. 'See that shiny bicycle – almost as good as these fine new bikes Uncle Quentin gave us!'

'Well, we can't stand here all day or we'll freeze to the spot!' said George. 'Come on – my mother wants her shopping done.'

She pushed open the shop door, and the cousins went in. It was bright and warm inside, and everything looked very Christmassy. The children went over to a counter with a good assortment of decorations. They chose some tinsel and prettily coloured glass balls for the tree, and a model of Father Christmas to go on top, as well as some gold and silver stars.

Julian went and paid for what they were buying.

But before they left the shop, George and her cousins wandered round looking — there were so many interesting things to see.

George spotted one of the shop assistants busy opening a cardboard carton in one corner of the shop. He was a young man called Bob. She knew him slightly. 'Hallo, Bob!' she said. 'Happy Christmas!'

The young man glanced up and smiled at the children.

'Hallo, kids! Doing some Christmas shopping?'

'Yes — we've been buying Christmas tree decorations for Aunt Fanny,' Dick told him.

Bob finished opening the carton. 'We've done a roaring trade in decorations this week,' he said. 'You'd be surprised how many people leave it till the last minute to buy tree decorations — like you! And the manufacturers are sometimes very late delivering our orders — that's a nuisance. For instance, we've been waiting a fortnight for these little bears, and they've only just arrived!'

As he spoke he lifted a box out of the big carton. There were two more boxes inside. Bob took the lid off the box, and showed the children that it was full of miniature teddy bears, all different colours: pink, blue, green, red, yellow, white, mauve and orange.

'Oh, aren't they sweet!' cried Anne, enchanted.

'I've never seen teddy bears used as Christmas

tree decorations before!' said Julian.

'Well, to tell you the truth,' Bob explained, 'they aren't really *meant* for Christmas trees. They're supposed to be mascots — the kind of thing you sometimes see hanging inside people's cars. There was quite a craze for them a little while ago. It's worn off now, but teddy bears are always popular, so these go on selling — and Mr Miles, my boss, decided to order some for Christmas and sell them as tree decorations.'

'And now they've been delivered too late! What a shame!' said George sympathetically. 'You'll never get rid of all those bears between now and Christmas Day! There must be an awful lot of them in the boxes.'

'Three dozen — thirty-six teddy bears in all. But don't worry! They're nice little bears, so I'm sure we'll sell them quite soon, even if they don't all go before Christmas. And I'll tell you something,' Bob added, smiling. 'Dr Thompson and his wife have ordered a dozen, so that's twelve sold already! Their little girl Jean is having a party for her friends this afternoon. It's a Christmas party, and they want the bears for their Christmas tree. I'd better go and telephone Dr Thompson and let him know his bears have come, so that he can pick them up.'

Dick smiled. 'Yes — we know Jean's having her friends to a party today,' he said. 'We've been invited too! Well, we'll be able to admire the bears on the tree ourselves. I should think they'd look rather good hanging there with the fairy lights and the other decorations.'

Anne, who was sometimes a little babyish for someone of ten, simply couldn't take her eyes off the little teddy bears. She picked one up to have a closer look at it. It was a blue bear with brown glass eyes which seemed to have a mischievous sparkle in them, and it had lovely soft fur. Anne stroked it.

'Oh, it's sweet!' she repeated.

Julian smiled at his little sister. He was very fond of Anne – she was so gentle and kind and sensible, always ready to do things for other people. He thought he'd like to give her a little treat.

'You keep that bear if you like it,' he said. 'I'll buy it for you.'

Anne flung her arms round Julian and gave him a big thank-you hug. While he was paying for the bear, someone called to Ben from the far end of the shop.

'Oh dear,' said the shop assistant, putting down the box of bears he was keeping for Dr Thompson. 'Now I won't have time to unpack the other twenty-three bears.'

'Would you like us to do it for you?' suggested George.

'No, that's all right, thank you all the same,

miss. I'll leave them in their carton until later – no, wait, I'll just put one in the window to attract customers. After all, we're staying open until five tomorrow. Goodbye, and have a nice time at your party!'

*　　*　　*

By four o'clock that afternoon, the party at the Thompsons' house was in full swing. Jean, the Thompsons' daughter, who was the same age as George and Dick, had gone to a lot of trouble to give her friends a really good time – and they *were* having a good time, all crowding round the Christmas tree. It was covered with mysterious parcels wrapped in pretty paper and tied with satin ribbon bows. The tree had fairy lights on it too, and tinsel and ornaments – including the twelve little teddy bears from the Kirrin Stores!

There was a table covered with delicious things to eat in one corner of the big room, and Jean was being a good hostess, making sure that everyone had what they wanted. 'More jelly, Paul? Molly, the little iced cakes are over there! Are you looking for the lemonade, Dick? Here it is – and here's a sugar lump for dear old Timmy too!'

When tea was over, Jean organised games. Musical Chairs was a great success, with everybody shouting and laughing.

'You cheated, Luke!'

'Just look who's talking! I saw *you* push Anne!'

'No, I didn't! She wasn't quite sitting down on the chair!'

Outside, night was falling, and soon it was really dark. The Christmas tree was sparkling with fairy lights.

'Now we're going to give the presents!' said Jean. The little girl took them off the tree, calling out the names of all her friends in turn.

'Mary, this looks rather like a nurse's uniform!' she said.

'Oh, how lovely! Just what I wanted!'

Dick and George both got roller-skates. 'Good!' said George cheerfully. 'Now we can both come a cropper at the same time!'

Julian had a penknife with several blades, and Anne's parcel held a little leather case full of sewing things. There was even a present for Timmy — a rubber bone!

Then all of a sudden, right in the middle of the party, the lights went out! Several of the girls screamed in alarm.

'Don't be scared,' said Julian in a calm voice. 'I expect it's only a blown fuse. Don't run about, or you may bump into things and hurt yourselves.'

In spite of Julian's good advice there was a lot of flurry and confusion in the room, but soon Dr Thompson's reassuring voice rose above the din.

'Just wait a minute, children! I'm going down to the cellar to mend the fuse.'

However, while Jean's father was gone people went on moving about in the dark. Dick, standing close to the door of the room, suddenly felt a draught — and then something scratchy brushed past his face. He took a step forward and bumped into a shadowy figure. Whoever it was pushed him away quite roughly.

'Hey, hold on!' said Dick indignantly. 'What do you think you're doing?'

At the same moment George, who was near Dick, realised that Timmy was dashing out of the room, and a few seconds later she heard him barking out in the garden.

'Hallo!' she thought. 'Someone must have left the front door open by mistake.'

Then Timmy's barking changed to a yowl of pain.

'*Timmy*!' cried George. 'He's been hurt!'

Just as she was going to run out of the room herself, the lights came on again, and Dr Thompson reappeared a moment later, smiling at his young guests. He was about to say something — when the smile froze on his lips! He was looking right over the children's heads with an expression of utter amazement in his eyes. The children themselves turned to look in the same direction — and *they* all exclaimed in surprise.

16

'The Christmas tree!'
'It's gone!'
'Wherever can it be?'
'Somebody's stolen it!'

Chapter Two

THE MISSING CHRISTMAS TREE

Imagine stealing a Christmas tree from a party – whoever heard of such a thing? All the same, Dr and Mrs Thompson and their guests had to admit that it had really happened. *Someone* must have taken the tree, because there was no denying that it had vanished without trace, and it couldn't just have flown away!

What was more, Dr Thompson had found out that the fuses down in the cellar were quite all right. Somebody had simply turned the electricity off at the main switch, so naturally all the lights went out. But who could have done it?

'Listen, Dr Thompson!' said George. 'My dog is still barking out in the garden – I bet he's after the thief!'

Everybody ran out of doors, with Dr Thompson

leading. Timmy was still there, sure enough —
apparently unhurt and barking angrily at the
closed garden gate. He sounded furious! And out
in the road a van was noisily starting off. Thanks to
the moonlight, Julian and George were just able to
make out the branches of a tree sticking out of the
back of the van.

'There go the people who stole the Christmas
tree!' cried George.

Then Dick remembered how something had
scratched his face as it was carried past him in the
dark. The Christmas tree, of course! But who
would have wanted to go to all that trouble? A
Christmas tree isn't really worth a great deal of
money — besides being a difficult thing to steal and
carry away. Dr and Mrs Thompson were asking
each other that very question. 'Why in the world
would anyone *want* to steal our tree?'

They told the children to go back indoors into
the warm, and then they telephoned Kirrin police
station to report the theft. A little later, two
policemen came to the house. They asked everyone
a lot of questions — and then went away again as
puzzled as the Thompsons and their guests! No
one could think why thieves would go to all that
trouble to steal something of such little real value.

When they were back at Kirrin Cottage, George
and her cousins spent most of the evening discuss-
ing what had happened at the party. The more

they thought about it the odder it seemed. They just couldn't make it out!

'Perhaps the thieves really wanted the *presents*, not the tree itself?' suggested Anne. 'They may not have known the parcels had already been taken off and given away.'

'I don't think that's very likely,' George told her. 'I mean, of course the presents were very nice, but they weren't all *that* valuable either. No, it looks as though the thieves had it all very carefully planned – they were after the tree, not the presents, and they got what they wanted.'

'But a Christmas tree is only an ordinary fir tree,' said down-to-earth Dick. 'You can't do anything much with it after Christmas.'

'I wonder if this particular tree *was* valuable for some other reason, though?' said Julian. 'Although I'll admit I can't think what that reason could be!'

When the four children went to bed that evening, all their unanswered questions were still going round and round in their heads. And they had a feeling that the incident of the stolen Christmas tree, ridiculous as it might seem, was the beginning of one of those mysteries that always seemed to be coming their way. They usually managed to solve the mysteries, too! All the same, this one did look remarkably puzzling.

* * *

And next morning there was yet another puzzle. George and her cousins were just about to sit down to a late but delicious breakfast of bacon, eggs and fried bread, when Aunt Fanny, who had gone into Kirrin to the baker's shop, came back with some lovely fresh rolls – and some interesting news. At about two that morning, burglars had broken into the Kirrin Stores.

'And the really odd thing is, nothing was stolen except a cardboard carton full of little teddy bears!' said Aunt Fanny. 'Oh yes – and a little bear just like the others which was on display in the window. Mr Miles says the police don't quite know what to make of it, but they think it was either a lunatic or a practical joker who broke into the shop!'

'How queer!' said George.

'Yes, it is, isn't it?' agreed Dick.

'Someone stole those teddy bears from the Kirrin Stores – and nothing else?' said Julian. 'That sounds pretty pointless!'

'A silly thing to do,' said Dick.

'No sillier than stealing Jean's Christmas tree,' George pointed out.

Anne suddenly thought of something! She said, in her soft little voice, 'Oh, do you remember? The little bears that the Thompsons had bought as Christmas tree decorations were still on the tree when it was stolen!'

Dick, Julian and George had just been thinking the very same thing.

'You're right, Anne,' said George. 'Well — maybe the lunatic at large in Kirrin is mad on teddy bears!'

It all sounded so ridiculous that the children didn't think it worth mentioning to anyone else. Anyway, Aunt Fanny was busy in the kitchen, cooking things for Christmas — wonderful spicy smells floated out to the children. And Uncle Quentin had gone off to shut himself up in his study as usual. Christmas or no Christmas, he was always deep in his scientific calculations.

Timmy seemed to want more of an explanation, though! 'Woof?' he asked.

'Well, what do *you* make of it, Timmy?' said Julian. 'You know,' he added thoughtfully, 'what George said certainly sounded silly, but it's worth bearing in mind. She could be right! Suppose the thief in both cases is a teddy bear collector — '

Dick interrupted his brother.

'Not *a* collector, old chap! There were at least two of them. It would have taken more than one person to pinch that Christmas tree and get it away and into the van so quickly.'

'And if you ask me,' said George, 'they didn't go stealing a Christmas tree from under our noses and then burgling the Kirrin Stores just to get hold of a lot of perfectly ordinary teddy bears!'

'Do you think there's something unusual about the bears themselves, George?' asked Julian, interested. 'Only we don't know what it is?'

'Well, yes — that's what I *do* think.'

'Hm — so the thieves, whoever they are, stole the bears on the tree *and* all the bears from the shop, including the one in the window display. They certainly knew where to go for them,' said Dick.

'They made a clean sweep, too — they stole every single bear,' said George.

'So now they've got the lot,' Dick agreed.

'No, they haven't!' Anne said suddenly. 'There's still *one* they haven't got — the one you gave me yesterday, Julian!'

'Goodness me — you're quite right!'

'Anne, go and fetch your little blue bear, quick!' said George.

So the little girl ran upstairs, and soon came down again with her little blue teddy bear 'mascot'.

Full of curiosity, the four children looked closely at it. Anne's bear didn't seem unusual in any way. It was just an ordinary, small soft toy, without anything special about it — or that was how it looked.

'Funny!' said Dick, shaking his head in bewilderment. 'And all the other bears were just like this one, too. Nice little bears, but nothing out of the ordinary.'

'It's interesting, all the same,' said George. 'I'm sure the two thefts are connected. Why don't we try to discover what it's all about?'

Of course the others agreed enthusiastically!

'Well, why don't we go back to the Kirrin Stores?' suggested Dick. 'We have to start making inquiries somewhere, and it might as well be there!'

'Okay,' said Julian, standing up. 'Come on, everyone! The shop will be open by now.'

And a moment later, four cyclists and a dog were on their way to Kirrin – and adventure!

Chapter Three

THE REPORTER

When the Five got to the Kirrin Stores they found several other people in the shop already, walking round and looking at the different counters. Some of them really did want to buy things, but some were just curious, and the three shop assistants were kept busy answering questions as they wrapped up parcels. Not surprisingly, everyone was talking about last night's burglary.

George saw Bob talking to a dark, stocky man of about forty. The man's eyes were hidden by dark glasses, and he looked as if he were a reporter. He was standing in a corner with Bob and taking down what the assistant told him in a notebook. The children went over, and Bob gave them a friendly smile.

'Hallo – back again? Do you want a few more Christmas decorations?'

'No, we just came out of curiosity!' George admitted.

The stranger in dark glasses seemed rather annoyed by this interruption.

'Never mind those kids,' he said to Bob, turning his back on the children. 'Now – where were we?'

'I've already told you all I know about the burglary, sir. The thieves didn't take anything except – '

'Yes, I know, except the coloured teddy bears!' the man interrupted him impatiently. 'But you still haven't answered my question. What I want to know is whether they took them *all*. Exactly *how many* bears did you have in the shop?'

'Twenty-four,' said Bob. George, who was extremely observant, thought she saw the stranger jump slightly, though he hid it well. Then he wrote the number down in his notebook. At the same moment, Bob met Anne's eyes, and he smiled. 'Oh no, I'm wrong!' he said. 'There were only twenty-three, because I sold one to this little girl yesterday!'

So far the man in dark glasses had not just ignored the children – he had looked as if he wished they weren't there at all! But now, all of a sudden, he turned very friendly.

'Well, well!' he said to Anne. 'So you bought one of those teddy bears, my dear? I'd heard that the burglars went off with the whole batch.'

'Yes, the whole batch except for the dozen already ordered by Dr Thompson, and a blue bear sold to this young lady,' Bob explained again. 'So there were just twenty-three bears stolen!'

The stranger was looking keenly at Anne.

'And you actually have one of the teddy bears, my dear?' he said. 'I'm writing about them for my paper, you know!'

'Are you?' said Anne rather timidly. But she took the toy out of her pocket and said, 'Here's my bear if you want to see him. Isn't he sweet?'

The reporter took the teddy bear, and seemed to be looking at it hard.

'Yes, very sweet!' he said at last, giving it back to Anne. 'Listen, little girl – how would you like to be in the newspaper? I might put *you* in my story too! Let's see if we can think of a good headline, shall we? *Blue Bear Survives Christmas Crime* – something like that?'

Julian, who didn't much care for the reporter's manner, took his sister's hand.

'Come along, Anne. Time we were going!' he said firmly.

'Just a moment, young man!' protested the man in dark glasses. 'I want to ask one or two more questions – for my paper, you understand! I have to fill up my column . . . ' And he asked Anne her name and address.

'Oh, I'm staying at Kirrin Cottage with my

27

Aunt Fanny and Uncle Quentin,' the little girl told him.

George, who was getting impatient, hoped the reporter would go away now and leave Anne alone. She had taken a dislike to him on sight — and besides, she was beginning to feel there was something odd about the questions he was asking. He seemed more interested in the number of stolen bears than anything else about the burglary! Why should that matter? It was strange.

'What newspaper do you write for?' George suddenly asked him.

The man snapped his notebook shut. 'The *News*,' he said. 'Well, now I must be off to write my story – goodbye!'

And he went out. Frowning, Dick muttered, 'The *News*? What *News*? The *Daily News*? The *Evening News*? The *Kirrin News*? That wasn't a full newspaper name he gave us! I don't like the look of him at all.'

'Nor do I!' said Julian – and *he* wasn't the sort of boy to make hasty judgements about people!

By now George, who wanted to get on with their own inquiries, was questioning Bob herself. But the children found out little more than they already knew. The burglars who had broken into the Kirrin Stores last night seemed to have known just where to find the burglar alarm, and they had cut the wires that would have set it off. Then they simply went off with the carton full of teddy bears and the one toy from the window display.

'That's the funniest thing about it!' Bob finished. 'It's odd enough for them to go stealing nothing but some toys which aren't really very valuable – we've got stuff here worth much more! But it's even odder that they took the trouble to steal the one from the window too. That certainly shows the thieves were only interested in the bears – *and* they had inside information! Or that's what the police think!'

'Odd? Yes – yes, it really is *extraordinary*,' George said slowly. She shook her head, and added, 'The disappearance of the Christmas tree from Jean's party was very odd as well. I do wonder what's behind all this!'

But some more last-minute Christmas shoppers came in and wanted Bob to serve them, so the children wished him a Happy Christmas again and went off. They obviously weren't going to get any further just at present – so they decided they might as well put the mystery out of their minds for a day or so and enjoy Christmas properly.

And enjoy it they certainly did – everyone at Kirrin Cottage had a lovely Christmas! Julian had said, trying not to sound gloomy, that he supposed he'd be too old for a Christmas stocking this year – but he had one too, as well as the other children. The fun of unpacking their stockings made the cousins forget all about the burglary at the Kirrin Stores. At one o'clock the whole family sat down to Christmas dinner. Aunt Fanny had decorated the table very prettily, and cooked a delicious meal of roast turkey with chestnut stuffing, roast potatoes and Brussels sprouts and bread sauce, followed by Christmas pudding and mince pies.

Dick had had three helpings of turkey! 'If you eat much more you'll have terrible indigestion!' George told him sternly – leaning over to take half his slice of Christmas pudding off his plate and put it on her own. But Dick's remaining half-slice turned out to be the one with a little silver charm in it!

After dinner they unwrapped their presents from the Christmas tree, laughing and talking happily. Uncle Quentin got a new jacket and Aunt Fanny had a very pretty dressing-gown. As for the children, George got a fine new pair of oars for her rowing boat, Julian was given a book that he'd been longing to read, there was a football for Dick, and Anne had a pretty outfit of clothes for her doll.

They admired each other's presents, and then the children went out for a walk by the sea, to get some fresh air. No one was very hungry for supper after so much Christmas dinner, so they only had a light meal, and then they played enthralling games of Scrabble and Consequences. They went to bed tired but very happy.

'I don't expect I'll want anything at all to eat tomorrow!' was the last thing Dick said to his brother before he went to sleep.

But strange to say, he did! The weather was beautiful on Boxing Day, cold but clear, and the children could spend the morning out of doors, playing in the garden and running races on the beach. So by dinner-time they had quite an appetite for cold turkey and ham with crisp fried potatoes and lots of salad. When Aunt Fanny looked at the remains of the turkey next morning, she realised that there was almost nothing left of it – and the rest of the food in her larder was running short too, so it was a good thing the shops were open again on December 27th! Aunt Fanny wrote out a shopping list and asked the children to take it into Kirrin village.

'These are all the things we need,' she said, showing them the list. 'Eggs, fruit, vegetables – I've written it all down. I think you'd better take two baskets. There'll be more than you can fit into your saddle-bags.'

So the Five set off to bicycle to Kirrin – or in Timmy's case to run there. The children always enjoyed a bicycle ride, so long as it wasn't raining, and the road was not too muddy. When they got to the village George did her mother's shopping, and the boys carried the baskets for her. There wasn't much left for Anne to do, so as she walked round

The Five set off to bicycle to Kirrin.

The woman looked excitedly at the little bear.

with the others she took her little teddy bear out of her pocket now and then and talked to it, or showed it to Timmy.

'Look, Timmy – don't you like my bear? What shall I christen him? I think I'll just call him Blue Bear!'

Suddenly a quiet voice behind Anne said, 'Oh, *what* a pretty bear! May I look at it?'

Anne turned round and saw a young woman smiling at her. The woman's eyes were rather sad – and she was holding out her hand for the bear.

Anne let her take it, and she saw that the woman's eyes were shining now, in quite an excited way. She seemed to be probing the bear's tummy with her fingers.

'My dear – I wonder, *would* you let me have this bear?' asked the woman in a breathless tone of voice. 'I'd pay you for it – pay you well! You see, I'd like it for my little boy. He's ill in bed, and I'm sure it would cheer him up!'

There was a pleading expression on her face now. Anne was a bit surprised by this sudden request, but the little girl had a very kind heart, and she was just going to say yes, when suddenly a hand came over her shoulder and firmly took the bear away from the woman again.

Chapter Four

THE SECRET OF THE BLUE BEAR

'I'm awfully sorry,' said George, politely but firmly, 'but my cousin has only just had this bear for a Christmas present! If you want one like it I should go to the Kirrin Stores. I'm sure they'll order one for you, and I don't suppose it will be long coming now that the Christmas rush is over.'

The woman started to protest, but George wasn't going to stop and listen! She pulled Anne away with her into the crowd of shoppers.

'Oh, George!' said Anne. 'Why wouldn't you let me give my bear to that lady? She only wanted it for her poor little boy who's ill!'

'Huh!' snorted George. 'I bet you anything she was making that up! She's been following us from Kirrin Cottage – didn't the rest of you notice? It's really amazing how many people are interested in those little teddy bears from the Kirrin Stores!'

'Whatever do you mean?' asked Julian in surprise. 'That woman *followed* us, did you say?'

'Yes — as we were leaving home I saw a small car parked up the road. It started up and then followed us at a distance, going very slowly to avoid passing us. It must have had to drive all the way to Kirrin village in second gear! In fact, it was *because* it was going at such a snail's pace that I noticed it. And then it did pass us at last, just as we got to the village. That woman was driving it. And then she popped up again as if by magic!'

'But why?' asked Dick. 'Do you think she's one of the "bear hunters" too?'

'It certainly looks like it. And I think that dark-haired man who was asking Bob questions on Christmas Eve is after the bears as well. Remember how keen he was to know just how many there were? *And* how interested he was to hear that Anne had one — the only bear that hadn't been stolen!'

Anne looked very startled. 'Goodness me!' she said. 'Yes, I see! Blue Bear is the only one left — and that's why the woman wanted to get hold of him!'

'Well, it's your own silly fault,' said Dick, unkindly. 'You were ass enough to give that reporter your address — if he *was* a reporter! I bet he's no more a reporter than I am. He probably told the woman to wait outside Kirrin Cottage, follow us when we came out, and try to soften Anne up!'

'And but for George she'd have done it, too,' said Julian.

George herself was looking thoughtful. 'Well – the thieves have failed in *this* attempt to get hold of Anne's Blue Bear. But I'm sure they'll try again,' she said.

'Aren't we going too fast?' said Dick. 'We could be imagining things, you know. There was certainly a burglary at the shop, that's a fact. And someone stole Jean's Christmas tree – that's another. However, we may be wrong to think the thieves were only after the teddy bears in the first place. And that woman *could* have been telling the truth!'

George looked at him rather impatiently. 'You want proof, do you, Dick?' she said. 'All right – we'll *find* proof! Let's go home and see what's inside Blue Bear!'

'Inside him?' asked Anne in surprise.

'Yes! I'll tell you my idea – I'm sure one of those teddy bears must have contained a secret. But the thieves have got thirty-five of the three dozen bears the shop ordered – all the bears but one! So if they're still trying to get hold of the thirty-sixth bear – Anne's bear – it means *that* bear is the right one! We'll get Blue Bear to tell us his secret.'

Quickly, the cousins finished their shopping and

then set off back to Kirrin Cottage. They were feeling slightly uneasy, and they kept looking back as they pedalled along to see if anyone was following. But no suspicious-looking cars seemed to be on the road.

However, it was with a sigh of relief that they came through the garden gate of Kirrin Cottage and closed it behind them. Phew! Safe home at last!

First of all the children took their shopping to the kitchen. Then, followed by Timmy, they went off to an old store-room which Uncle Quentin had had made into a games room for them. It was right at the other end of the house from his study! Uncle Quentin couldn't stand noise when he was trying to do his important scientific work – and when he heard that Julian, Dick and Anne were coming for Christmas, he realised that the four children wouldn't be able to play out of doors as much as they did in the summer. So he thought he had better give them a place where they *could* shout and laugh and make a noise, and still not disturb him! It was an arrangement that suited everyone.

Once the children were safely on their own, Anne took Blue Bear out of her pocket.

'Woof!' said Timmy, looking interested.

'It's quite a small toy,' said Dick, taking the little bear from his sister. 'I don't see what could be hidden inside it.'

'A diamond, perhaps?' suggested Anne.

'Or more likely a piece of paper,' said George, picking up the bear and feeling it in her turn. 'Wait a minute – yes, when I press hard I think I *can* feel something like paper crackling right inside the bear!'

'Well, let's have a look,' said Julian, producing the lovely new penknife he had got at Jean's party. 'Here goes! Julian Kirrin the world-famous surgeon is now about to perform a breathtakingly skilful operation!'

But in his haste to find out what was in the bear, Julian fumbled with it and dropped it. Both Dick and George put out a hand to catch it as it fell – and their hands collided, knocking the bear up into the air again! Timmy thought this looked like a splendid game of ball, and he couldn't resist the temptation to join in the fun. He jumped up and caught the teddy bear in his mouth.

'Oh – my bear!' cried Anne.

'Drop it, Timmy!' George ordered. She grabbed Timmy's collar, and Dick tried to get the toy away from him. But thinking this was all part of the game, Timmy kept his jaws firmly closed. In fact he clamped them together even *more* firmly, and pretended to growl fiercely, as much as to say that he would defend his prey against all comers!

'That'll do, Timmy!' said George sternly. 'Drop it! Give it to me.'

'Drop it, Timmy!' George ordered.

A tightly folded piece of paper fell out into Julian's hand.

But it was too late! Dick and Timmy were both tugging so hard at the toy, in different directions, that something was bound to give way. The seam down the teddy bear's back suddenly tore open.

Taken by surprise, Timmy let go at last, and Dick picked Blue Bear up. The four children leaned over to look at the open seam. They couldn't see anything but stuffing. Then Anne put her little finger inside the gap.

'Oh, I can feel something!' she said.

Julian carefully rolled back the edges of the open seam, turned the teddy bear upside down – and a piece of tightly folded paper fell out into the palm of his hand.

For a moment or so the children stood there motionless, looking at their find. Blue Bear had told them his secret!

'Well, it was a pretty good hiding place,' George said at last. 'Now to find out what this piece of paper *is*!'

Julian was already unfolding it. George, Dick and Anne stood watching him silently, in suspense. Julian smoothed out the paper, and they all bent over it.

They saw a number of rectangular shapes neatly drawn on the paper in black ink. The lines formed a kind of sketch, and there were a few figures and letters written in too.

'It's a plan!' cried Dick excitedly.

'So *this* is what they were after!' said Julian thoughtfully.

No one asked him who 'they' were. They all knew he meant the thieves who had stolen the Christmas tree from under the noses of Jean's party guests, and had then burgled the shop too.

'Well, we were right!' said George, very pleased. '*Now* do you believe me, Dick? The thieves *were* after Blue Bear!'

'Poor little bear!' said Anne sadly. 'He looks as if someone had stabbed him in the back!'

'He'll be all right, Anne,' said George, with a quick glance at the toy. 'It's only the seam. You know how good you are at sewing – get a needle and thread, and you'll have him cured again in no time!'

While Anne was busy mending her little bear, George and the boys looked more closely at the plan. It was a rather disappointing find really, after all. Dick was the first to say so.

'It's a plan all right – but a plan of what? I can't make head or tail of it! We've got no idea what it's about, and there isn't a single clue to tell us, either!'

'We won't give up yet,' said Julian. 'It might be the plan of a house – '

'Or maybe it shows where a treasure's hidden on a desert island!' suggested George, whose imagination was always apt to run away with her.

Just then the Five heard Aunt Fanny calling from the kitchen.

'Dinner's ready, children!'

Anne cut off her thread. 'There!' she said, looking at her work. '*That's* done – and Blue Bear is almost as good as new.'

'We can take another look at the plan after dinner,' said Dick. 'But meanwhile we ought to hide it. Where shall we put it?'

'Woof!' said Timmy, as if in answer to the question.

'Yes, Timmy dear, that's a very good idea!' said George, laughing. 'Timmy says we ought to give *him* the plan – it'll be safe as houses in his kennel.'

She hurried to find an envelope and some drawing pins. They put the plan inside the envelope, and then fixed it to the inside of the roof of Timmy's kennel with the drawing pins.

'And now we'd better hurry,' said George. 'My father doesn't like us to be late for meals.'

But luckily Uncle Quentin was a little late for dinner himself that day, so the children didn't get scolded. And they had a good appetite for dinner now that they felt they had the advantage over their mysterious opponents!

Chapter Five

ANOTHER THEFT

The weather was still fine that afternoon. The Five would have liked snow best of all, but although there was no sign of any snow yet the day was clear, bright and dry, and they thought they should take advantage of it to be out of doors.

'Let's got for a bicycle ride,' said George. 'We can go back to puzzling out that plan this evening – there's no special hurry!'

Anne didn't want to be parted from Blue Bear, so she put him in the saddle-bag of her bicycle. Julian shook his head rather doubtfully.

'Don't you think it's a bit risky to take him too?' he asked. 'They've tried to get him away from you once already . . . '

'Yes – and now Blue Bear will make very good bait!' George pointed out. 'We just have to keep an eye on him – and with luck we'll catch our friends red-handed trying to steal him! Then we'll know who they are.'

'What a good idea!' said Anne. 'All we have to do is keep a careful watch – though we mustn't *look* as if that's what we're doing.'

'I hope the thieves do take the bait!' said Dick. 'Then we'll follow them to their hiding place, and tell the police, and they'll be caught and –'

'We're nowhere near that stage yet, chatterbox!' put in Julian, getting on his bicycle. 'Come on, everyone! Race you all to the wood!'

When they reached the little wood on the far side of Kirrin village, the children stopped to have a rest and get their breath back. But it was too cold to stand around for long, so they were soon off again.

On their way back, Anne wanted to stop and go into a nice little shop which had just opened in the village. It was run by a clever man who carved pretty things out of wood and then sold them in his shop. The children left their bicycles leaning against the shop front and went in, with Timmy. They admired the things the man had made – salad bowls, wooden spoons and forks, toys and models, bead necklaces and so on. Julian bought a little wooden bowl as a present for Aunt Fanny.

The Five went out of the shop again – and as soon as they were outside Anne could see that someone had been meddling with her bicycle. Its saddle-bag was wide open.

'Oh!' she cried. 'Blue Bear!'

She searched the saddle-bag, but it was no good: the little toy had gone.

George bit her lip in annoyance. 'It's my fault!' she said. 'I was the first to say we must keep a good watch for anyone trying to steal that bear – and then I went and forgot! Somebody must have been spying on us. Maybe we were followed all the way from Kirrin Cottage! Oh, *bother* – why didn't I think of leaving Timmy on guard out here with the bikes?'

'It's *all* our faults,' said Julian. 'Still, who'd have thought anyone would go to the trouble of following us all this way? I didn't *see* anything at all suspicious, either!'

'Nor did I,' Dick agreed with him.

George and Anne had not noticed anything either! But when she thought about it, George did remember hearing a motorbike stop somewhere near, while they were inside the shop.

'That must have been the thief,' she said gloomily. 'Oh, I could kick myself for being so careless!'

The Five didn't often do anything so silly – that was why they so often managed to solve the complicated mysteries they came across. But the theft of Anne's teddy bear was specially annoying because it cut off the line of inquiry which they had hoped might lead them to the enemy.

'What shall we do now?' Julian wondered.

'We could go to the police,' suggested Anne. 'After all, my teddy bear *has* been stolen!' ·

'Go to the police?' said Dick. 'And tell them what? Tell them someone stole a toy worth about fifty pence? They'd just laugh at you, Anne!'

'They wouldn't laugh if we told them what we suspect and showed them the plan!' said Anne.

'But we don't want to tell them about the plan!' George protested. 'Then we'd have to hand it over to the police, and goodness knows when we'd get it back. Or even *if* we'd get it back! After all, it does belong to you, Anne, since it was inside your bear. As for our suspicions, you know, I've got a nasty feeling the police wouldn't take them seriously.'

Perhaps her arguments weren't very convincing, but then her cousins didn't particularly want to be convinced! They all felt that the mystery of the teddy bears was *their* mystery, and they wanted to solve it all on their own. The only trouble was that just now, the prospects of doing that didn't look very good!

Standing by the roadside with their bicycles, the children discussed the situation for a minute or so more before starting off again. And suddenly George cheered up!

'I say – it's all right after all,' she said. 'I've thought of something. Our link with the thief isn't broken yet! Now I come to think of it, whoever stole Blue Bear will be busy at this very moment looking inside him – just as *we* did this morning!'

'Yes, of course,' said Dick, rather grumpily.

'And he'll soon see that the seam down the back came open and has been sewn up again,' George went on.

'So what?'

'Oh yes – I see!' put in Julian, excitedly. 'The thief will open up the bear again and – '

'And when he searches its inside, he won't find anything there!' George finished. 'So he'll work it out that we've found whatever was hidden inside the bear, and it's in our hands!'

'Yes, I never thought of that!' cried Anne happily. 'The thief will soon be after us again – and this time, so long as we remember to keep our eyes open a bit better, we really ought to spot him!'

However, George herself was looking less cheerful now. She frowned as she thought out loud.

'There's just one thing,' she said. 'Unless he's going to search Kirrin Cottage from top to bottom – and I don't see *how* he could do that – I don't know how he'd set about getting hold of the plan.'

'My word!' Julian suddenly sounded worried too. 'Suppose he intends to kidnap one of us and get the information out of him – or her – by force?'

Dick set his jaw, looking quite fierce.

'We'll just have to stick close together and make

sure we don't get separated!' he said. 'And with a guard dog like Timmy we should be safe enough!'

'Perhaps whoever's stolen Blue Bear will get in touch with us by telephone, or write to us?' suggested Anne.

'But I wonder how he'd think he could *make* us give him the plan? said George. 'Still, I agree with you – he certainly *will* try to get in touch. And then it'll be up to us to outwit him!'

And the Five went back to Kirrin Cottage, feeling a little better about it all.

*   *   *

However, though the children were on tenterhooks waiting for something to happen, nothing *did* happen the next day. And hard as they tried to make sense of the plan, it was still a perfect mystery to them.

On the afternoon of December 29th, the sun was shining so brightly that the children and Timmy went down to the beach for a game of ball. The sea was calm, and the sand felt quite warm in the sun. They hardly needed their winter coats!

They had some fine games. There was nobody else on the beach, so they could shout as loud as they liked. Timmy joined in too, running after the ball and pushing it with his nose whenever he managed to get it. He looked so funny bounding about that he made the children laugh.

They were enjoying their game so much that none of them heard the noise of a motorbike which stopped abruptly on the road above the beach.

Timmy was the first to realise that they were not alone any more. He was usually a very friendly dog, even with strangers — but today, for some strange reason, he immediately stopped playing and stood there perfectly still, legs rigid, showing his teeth and growling quietly to himself.

George was surprised. She turned round — and saw an unexpected figure standing there, only a few feet away from them.

Chapter Six

THE MOTOR-CYCLIST

The motor-cyclist coming towards the children looked quite a young man. Not that they could see much of him — he wore tall boots, and a motor-cyclist's helmet with a tinted visor, and there was a scarf wound round his neck and chin, hiding the lower part of his face.

Altogether he looked rather sinister, perhaps because you couldn't make out his features. And then there was Timmy's unusual behaviour — his instinct never let him down, as the four children well knew. That made them feel uneasy as well. Anne came a little closer to Julian, as if she wanted him to protect her. Dick, who had been about to throw the ball, lowered his arm. He wasn't sure what to do next.

'Hallo, kids!' said the newcomer, moving closer. 'Enjoying the sunshine, eh?'

He spoke in a jovial tone which sounded false. There was something the children didn't like one little bit about his voice.

'Yes,' said Dick gruffly. 'It's a fine day, and so—'

'And so where's that paper?' the stranger rudely interrupted him.

Dick was taken aback, and Julian replied instead. 'Paper? What paper?'

'You needn't pretend – you know quite well what I mean! The paper you found inside the bear.'

George spoke up boldy. 'We don't know what you're talking about,' she said firmly. 'As for my cousin's bear, some nasty mean sneak-thief stole it yesterday. If you don't believe me just ask Anne here! It was her bear, and she's still very upset about it, poor thing!'

She pointed to Anne, who nodded, feeling scared. The motor-cyclist looked hard at George.

'Now listen to me, my lad!' he said, thinking George was a boy. 'You've got a quick tongue, but I'm not swallowing that story, so don't you think you can fool me! The bear *may* have been stolen, but the plan wasn't inside it any more, so that means *you've* got it!'

George and Dick exchanged meaningful glances. This young man talked too much, and he had just given himself away! If he knew the bear was empty, that meant that either he'd stolen it

51

The motor-cyclist coming towards them looked rather sinister.

himself, or it had been stolen by an accomplice of his. And he had said *plan*, not just *paper* – so that strange drawing *was* a plan. The children had thought so, but they hadn't been absolutely sure until now.

Well, here they were face to face with one of the enemy. They'd hoped to make contact with the people who stole the teddy bears, and they had! The important thing now was to play a clever game and hang on to their advantage, as the children quickly realised.

But Timmy, who was only a dog, if a very intelligent one, acted on instinct. All *he* knew was that there was a threatening stranger here on the beach – and his instinct told him it was his duty as a good dog to chase the man away.

So Timmy went into action. He attacked! Before the man knew what was happening, the dog's teeth had closed on his right leg. Luckily for him, his thick leather boot kept him from being really hurt. However, he was furious and frightened.

'You brute!' he shouted. And taking a kind of cosh out of his pocket, he brought it down with a crack on poor Timmy's head. Timmy was knocked unconscious and fell to the ground without so much as a whimper. He lay there without moving.

'Timmy!' cried George, falling to her knees on the sand beside him. 'How *dare* you touch my dog?' she shouted at the man. 'You'll be sorry for this if you've killed him!'

'Go easy, kid!' said the man. 'And stop yelling like that, unless *you* want a knock on the head too!'

Julian and Dick, boiling with indignation, both stepped forward. 'And you others keep quiet too!' the man told them. He waved his cosh in their faces. 'I didn't come here to play about – I want to ask you some questions. So let's start again! What did you do with the paper you found inside that toy bear?'

The boys said nothing. George, who was not taking any more notice of what was going on, scooped up some water from a rock pool and sprinkled it over Timmy's nose. Poor little Anne was sniffing hard, trying not to cry – and next moment the motor-cyclist turned to *her*!

'Since your friends won't talk, *you* can tell me what I want to know, little girl. And mind you tell the truth! Well, where's that paper?'

Anne looked round her in desperation – but there were no grown-ups to come to their aid. She was trembling. 'I – I haven't got the paper!' she stammered. 'I mean, we haven't got it here, it – it's hidden in my uncle's house!' And summoning up all her courage, she lifted her chin defiantly and added, 'Even if you break into Kirrin Cottage and search the whole place you'll never, never find it! It's far too well hidden.'

Poor Anne! She thought that if she said that the

man would give up, and there would be no more danger to Kirrin Cottage or anyone living there. So she was horrified when the motor-cyclist just burst out laughing.

'Ho, ho, ho – *that's* a good 'un!' he said sarcastically. 'Do you really think I'd go to all that trouble and risk getting caught? What a hope!'

Then he turned serious again – and he sounded dangerous.

'No, no – you kids are going to be good children and give me that paper. Soon, too! I'll give you until tomorrow. You must leave the plan here on the beach by twelve noon – put it underneath that rock.'

And he showed them his cosh again, adding, 'If you breathe a word of this to the police or your parents you'll be sorry! It'll be the worse for you if you don't leave the plan here for me. Oh yes, you'll be *very* sorry!'

He might sound melodramatic, but all the same, George and her cousins felt sure his threat was serious. The motor-cyclist meant what he said – he wasn't joking!

'Well – do you understand?' he asked.

'Yes!' said Dick. 'You'll get your plan – and I hope it chokes you!' he added under his breath.

The motor-cyclist put his cosh back in his pocket. 'Twelve noon tomorrow. Don't forget!' he repeated.

Then he turned round and went up the path from the beach and back to the road again. Julian, Dick and Anne stood there watching him go. George was still kneeling beside poor Timmy, who was beginning to come round. 'Oh yes, he'll get his plan!' she muttered grimly. 'And much good it'll do him – because it won't be worth anything.'

Hearing her, Dick looked at her in a puzzled way. 'What do you mean, George?'

'I mean we're going to give him a fake plan, of course!' she said. 'You don't think I'm idiotic enough to let him have the real thing, do you?'

'Oh, listen!' said Anne.

Over on the road, just out of sight, they heard a motorbike starting up.

'So his motor-cyclist's gear wasn't just camouflage,' said Dick. 'I thought it might be, but he really does go about on a motorbike.'

The four children didn't feel like going on with their game now, and in any case George wanted to get Timmy back to Kirrin Cottage. Her poor dog would need a good meal and a nice sleep in the warm, before he felt quite better again.

'Come on, old boy,' she told him. 'Good, brave Timmy! If that brute hadn't knocked you out you'd have made mincemeat of him, wouldn't you?'

'And then put him in mince pies,' said Dick, laughing.

'Woof,' said Timmy doubtfully. He wasn't very fond of mince pies!

* * *

Back at Kirrin Cottage, the children made Timmy comfortable in his basket at the foot of George's bed, and then they held a meeting. Dick went to fetch the plan from the kennel. He spread it out on the table in the games room.

'George said we could give the man a fake plan,' he remarked, 'but it's still got to *look* genuine.'

'Yes,' agreed Julian. 'If we draw just any old sketch out of our heads, I don't think he and his friends will be deceived for a moment. And then they'll be after us again.'

'For a start, we ought to use the same sort of paper if possible,' said Anne, sensibly.

'I thought of that too!' said George, smiling. 'Luckily it'll be easy – this sheet of paper obviously came from an exercise book, like the ones we use for rough work at school. And I've got several spare rough books in this drawer. As for the plan itself – '

'It must look real, remember!' repeated Dick.

'Oh, it'll *look* real all right. Listen – I've had an idea! We'll trace the plan, but the wrong way round!'

Dick looked admiringly at his cousin. 'I say!

That *is* a brilliant idea, George!' he exclaimed.

Julian went over to look at the plan, and nodded. 'Yes, that should work all right,' he said. He tore a sheet of paper out of one of George's exercise books and went over to the window, where he would have a good light for tracing the plan. He got a piece of tracing paper and a pen. 'It's easy enough to *do* it,' he said as he worked. 'The hard part was *thinking* of it. Well done, George!'

After a few minutes' work, Julian had traced the original plan on the new piece of paper, but back to front like a mirror image.

'There!' he said, satisfied. 'It looks fine – only it's the wrong way round!'

'Yes,' said Dick excitedly. 'I call that a stroke of genius! The thieves may be completely taken in – but even if they aren't and they suspect there's something wrong, we'll still have gained time!'

'What about the numbers and letters?' asked Anne in her soft little voice.

'Numbers and letters?'

'The ones written in on the plan! Look! – where it says N and S and E and W! That must mean North, South, East and West. And then there are some figures too.'

'My word, I nearly forgot them!' said Julian. He scribbled a few figures on the back-to-front plan, the first that came into his head, and then added the letters at random. No one would be able to make head or tail of the plan now!

'Well,' said George, 'all we have to do now is keep watch when the motor-cyclist comes to pick it up. We won't be able to follow him on our bikes, of course — but at least we can take down the number of his motor-bike, and that should be a good clue. Who knows — it may even lead us to his friends, and help us to find out what's really behind the mystery of those little teddy bears!'

Chapter Seven

AN EXPEDITION TO MIDDLETON

Next morning the Five went down to the beach at about ten o'clock. The motor-cyclist had told them to leave the plan there by twelve noon, so it didn't sound as if he would be there himself to pick it up earlier than twelve o'clock. However, with his usual common sense Julian said he thought they'd better act as if they might be being watched the whole time.

They took the path down to the beach quite openly, without trying to hide. George was carrying the fake plan, protected by a plastic bag. The beach was deserted, just as it had been the day before, and she put the 'plan' underneath the rock. Then the children went straight back to Kirrin Cottage.

But as soon as the garden gate had closed behind

the Five, George cried, 'Quick – hurry!' And they put the second part of the operation into action! Racing across the garden, they went round the corner of the house and out by the back gate, which opened into a lane with tall banks on either side.

Even going the long way round, it didn't take them more than a few minutes to get back to the road running along the shore above the beach.

'Where can we hide?' asked Anne.

There was a small shelter by the bus stop, a little way down the road, and George pointed to that.

'Behind the bus shelter!' she said. 'The motorcyclist must have left his bike somewhere near here yesterday.'

George had told Timmy to keep quiet, and he followed the children in silence. It was not the first time he'd been a watchdog, and he was well trained to obey George and do whatever she told him!

For quite a long time nothing at all happened. Then the twelve o'clock bus came along the road, and went straight on to Kirrin without stopping. The bus stop was a request one, and nobody wanted to get on or off the bus there today.

'We must start watching extra hard now!' said Dick. 'It's twelve – our friend will be showing up any moment!'

'Friend, did you say?' inquired Julian.

'Well, friend or foe, we must keep a good lookout for him anyway!' said Dick, laughing. 'Oh, look – here comes a motorbike!'

But the motorbike went on along the road. A coach followed it a few minutes later. Then there was a lorry, and then . . .

'Watch out!' cried George. She had a good view of the road. 'Here he comes!'

The Five were hiding behind the shelter, making themselves as small and inconspicuous as possible. The noise of the motorbike's engine grew louder – and then stopped. The children didn't dare risk looking yet. They waited a moment, and at last Dick stuck his head out of hiding.

'Yes, there's the motorbike!' he whispered. 'He stopped on the other side of the road, right beside the cliff above the beach. Let's go and see what he's doing!'

They crossed the road, keeping very quiet, and the George went down flat on her stomach. Taking all the precautions she could, she crawled to the very edge of the cliff.

One glance was enough to show her the motorcyclist going down the path to the beach.

'He's on his way to pick up the plan,' she told the others. 'Come on – we haven't got much time!'

Then the four children moved very fast! While Dick was carefully copying down the registration number of the motorbike's number plate, and Anne and Timmy kept watch, George and Julian hastily searched the carriers of the motorbike. They were hoping to find some clue that would tell them who the young man was.

And luck was on their side! Julian found a letter with a name and address on the envelope. 'A pity it doesn't say who sent it, too!' grumbled George, taking down the details. However, the main thing was that it was addressed to Mr Simeon Ruddock, Middleton, near Kirrin.

Julian put the envelope back where he had found it – and only just in time!

'Woof!' barked Timmy quietly, to let them know someone was coming along the road. 'Woof!'

'Watch out!' Anne whispered at the same time. She was watching the beach too. 'The motor-cyclist's coming back!'

And the Five walked away as fast as they could, but looking as casual as possible.

Once they were back at Kirrin Cottage they put their heads together.

'We didn't really get *much* information!' said Julian glumly. He was inclined to look on the dark side at times.

'You can't mean that, Ju!' cried George. '*I* think we've had a tremendous stroke of luck! If all we'd got to help us was the number of the motorbike, it might have taken us sometime to find out who the owner is. But that envelope made us a present of his name and address!'

However, Julian shook his head. 'We can't be sure that he's Simeon Ruddock. He may be going about on a motorbike he's stolen or borrowed, and that letter was sent to its real owner,' he pointed out.

'Oh, come on, Julian – don't be so depressing! You must admit it's far more likely the bike and the letter *do* both belong to him than that they *don't*!'

'Yes, I suppose so,' Julian agreed.

'Well, then, let's act on the assumption that they *are* his,' said George. 'And if we're wrong, we'll still have time to change our tactics.'

'I think George is right,' said Dick.

'Yes – do let's try to find out more,' Anne said earnestly.

But then they were interrupted by Aunt Fanny, calling out that it was dinner time. They had to go off to the dining-room.

'Right – we'll go into Middleton this afternoon!' George decided as they left the games room. 'The village isn't very far from Kirrin. It looks as if it's beginning to drizzle, but a little bit of water won't hurt us!'

Yes, it would certainly have taken more than a spot of rain to stop the Five in the very middle of an adventure! And in fact the rain stopped early in the afternoon, just before they reached Middleton. Poor Timmy was glad of that. He didn't like getting his coat wet and his paws muddy.

The children left their bicycles just outside Middleton, and were on their way into the village on foot when Timmy saw a big Alsatian dog coming towards him. The other dog sniffed him in a superior sort of way.

'Grrr!' said the Alsatian.

Which Timmy quite correctly took to mean, 'What on earth is this strange dog doing in *my* village?'

Timmy replied. 'Woof!' in the same tone — meaning, 'If you don't like the look of me, *I* don't like the look of *you* either!'

'Grr! Ugly mongrel!' barked the other dog.

The furious Timmy replied with a string of horrible insults — in dog language, of course! It sounded as if he were challenging the Alsatian.

'Grrrrr!'

And before George had time to realise what was happening, the two dogs went for each other. Soon all you could make out was a big ball of brown and grey hair whirling about in the middle of the muddy road, making a dreadful yowling, yapping noise!

Hearing it, several of the villagers came out on their doorsteps. Julian felt cross. He would have far preferred the Five to arrive in a less conspicuous way. George was trying to call Timmy off, but it was no good. The fighting dogs didn't even hear her! People came crowding round

Anne and Timmy kept watch while the others searched for a clue to the motor-cyclist's identity.

People came crowding round to watch the two dogs fighting.

to watch, talking and laughing.

'My money's on the big Alsatian – he's a good deal heavier!'

'That's Matt's dog, Wolf. He'll murder the other one, that he will!'

'Oh no!' cried poor George, alarmed.

'Well, *I'd* bet on the smaller dog myself,' said someone else. 'He's tough – and see what spirit he's got!'

'Hey, here comes Matt!' said a boy.

And a tall, strong man came striding up.

'My word!' he exclaimed. 'Did you ever? I've never seen my Wolf get the worst of a fight before – this is certainly the first time! Well, I'll be blowed!'

And laughing jovially, the big man fearlessly tackled the yowling, scuffling dogs, taking each of the two animals by the scruff of the neck and yanking them apart.

'Well, well! If you've *quite* finished your fight . . .!'

George hurried up to claim Timmy. Matt, still laughing, went off with his own dog, who didn't much want to go! George took stock of the damage to Timmy.

He wasn't as badly hurt as she had feared at first, though one of his ears was bleeding, and there were a few tufts of hair missing here and there.

'Don't worry, George – he'll live!' said Dick, trying to reassure his cousin.

'We must do something about that torn ear,

though,' said George, concerned. 'It ought to be disinfected. I wonder if there's a chemist's shop in this village?'

Just then two boys who had been watching the dog-fight came up to the children. They were smiling in a friendly way.

'Can we help?' the bigger boy asked George. 'I say – it was awfully brave of your dog to tackle Wolf, the big Alsatian! My name's Thomas, and this is my brother Giles. We live quite close – why don't you come home with us, and we'll get out the surgical spirit and clean your dog's sore places up?'

George thought this was a very good idea. Thomas and Giles's parents were out, but the two boys found what they needed in the bathroom medicine cupboard. Timmy, who had been so brave in the heat of battle, was rather a coward when it came to disinfecting his bleeding ear, so it all took quite a time.

The four cousins saw their opportunity to find out more about what they wanted to know, and they asked their new friends some questions, getting round to the subject of the motor-cyclist in rather a clever way!

'This looks like a nice village,' Dick began. 'And the people seem nice, too!'

'Yes,' said George. 'They did seem kind – even Matt smiled when he saw the way Timmy went for his huge dog!'

'We did meet *one* person here we didn't like, though,' Julian put in. 'I wonder if you know him? He was on a motorbike, and he jolly nearly ran us down. Quite a young man – we didn't get a chance to see his face, but the thing is that as he passed something dropped off his bike and we picked it up. It was a little package addressed to Simeon Ruddock. I suppose we really ought to find him and return it to him.'

'Simmy Ruddock?' exclaimed Giles. 'I'm not surprised you didn't like him – we don't either! He's horrible.'

Chapter Eight

AN INTERESTING CONVERSATION

'Oh, do you know him?' asked Anne eagerly. 'Simmy Ruddock, I mean.'

'Everyone in Middleton knows him,' said Thomas. 'You might say he was the black sheep of the village! But if you go to his house you're not very likely to find him at home. He spends most of his time out and about, usually up to no good! He lives with his elder brother – *he's* all right, and he gets very upset about the way Simmy behaves!'

'Where do you think we *could* find Simmy, then?' asked George.

'Well,' said Thomas, 'if he isn't roaring around the country on his motorbike, you'll probably find him at the Grand Café in the High Street. He spends a lot of time there.'

'There's nothing very *grand* about the place either, except its name.' Giles explained. 'All the worst characters in Middleton meet there. Simmy always says he's looking for a job and he goes to the Grand Café because he might meet somebody useful there – though *that's* hardly likely! He does work now and then, but he never stays long in any job. My father says Simmy doesn't really like work.'

'How will we recognise him if we do find him at the Grand Café?' asked Julian. 'We've seen him in his motor-cyclist's gear, but we didn't get a proper look at his face.'

'Oh, he has a thin, sallow sort of face – and a harsh, rather high voice like a door when its hinges need oiling!'

The cousins smiled at this description. Then they said thank you to Thomas and Giles, and set off again.

'Let's go and take a look at this Grand Café, then,' suggested Julian. 'Maybe we'll find our bird roosting there!'

'Funny sort of bird he is, too!' said Dick. 'Keeps on changing his job, and spends the rest of his time in this shady-sounding café! I'm not a bit surprised to find he's hand in glove with whoever did that burglary.'

Middleton was not a very large place, and it had only two cafés. The Grand Café looked dirty and dilapidated, and there was a loud racket coming from a jukebox inside it. The children saw

Simmy's motorbike parked outside, and they stopped, wondering just what to do next.

'It's no good looking in through the window,' said George thoughtfully. 'If Simmy catches sight of us, that puts an end to our hopes of finding out any more.'

'Why not wait hidden behind a car on the other side of the road?' suggested Dick. 'We know he's in there, so he's bound to come out in the end. And if he's with anyone else –'

'Ssh!' whispered Anne. 'Here he comes!'

As soon as the children saw the young man who was coming out of the café, they knew they were right about his identity. No doubt about it – this was the motor-cyclist in helmet and boots who had gone off with the fake plan! He was carrying his helmet now. His face fitted the description Thomas and Giles had given them. And he had a companion – a dark, stocky man of about forty, who followed him out into the road. Dick recognised him straight away.

'It's the man who was wearing dark glasses!' he whispered. 'The one who said he was a reporter, and asked Bob all those questions about the burglary at the Kirrin Stores!'

Julian, George and Anne recognised him too.

'That means those two must be in league with each other,' said Julian. 'They certainly *look* like conspirators!'

'What a pity we can't hear what they're saying!' sighed Anne.

'I've got an idea!' whispered George. 'Look — they've stopped beside Simmy's motorbike to talk. If they're going to stay there for any length of time, we *can* hear at least some of what they're saying.'

'But how?'

'Follow me, and you'll find out!' said George.

Stooping low, so that the parked cars would hide her, George set off down the pavement to the end of the road.

'Now let's cross, very cautiously, and go along *that* road — the one opposite.'

Julian, Dick and Anne did as George said, though they didn't see what her idea was. They crossed the road quite a long way from the two men, who were deep in conversation and didn't even look in their direction.

'And now let's go round the corner here,' said George, 'and this alley will lead us back to the café! It stands on the corner of the alley and the High Street — I spotted the alley from where we were just now!'

Sure enough, the children and Timmy found themselves just round the corner from Simmy and his friend. They stopped and listened. They couldn't see the two men, but they could hear quite a lot of what they were saying.

'All right, you say? Huh!' snorted the stocky

The two conspirators were deep in conversation.

man. He sounded cross about something. 'If you hadn't bungled everything at the start –'

'It wasn't my fault, Leo!' said Simmy, in his rather high, harsh voice.

'Keep your voice down, will you? Come over this way!'

The children flattened themselves against the wall where they were standing. After all their trouble, they were disappointed to see the two men walk past them and go away, still talking!

'Let's follow,' whispered Dick. 'We may still find out more.'

And yet again the children were in luck! Simmy and the other man stopped close to a patch of waste land in a lonely spot. There was a fence on one side of it, cutting it off from a building site where a house was being put up. Simmy lit a cigarette, his friend lit a pipe, and they both started talking again.

Once more the Five carefully skirted round their quarry – and soon they were crouching behind the fence. This time they could hear what the men were saying quite clearly.

'I tell you, Leo, I couldn't help it!' Simmy protested. 'How was I to know the delivery would be late? My job ended just before they came in!

'Okay – I'll admit that was bad luck. Because you left just then, we had to mount a pretty risky operation, and then a break-in, all to get hold of that delivery! Ridiculous!'

'Well, everything's worked out, that's what matters,' said Simmy. 'You've got the plan now! If we follow its instructions we'll soon get our hands on the goods! Then all we have to do is get 'em out of the country and dispose of them – which ought to be a very profitable deal!'

'Don't forget we'll have to put Roddy's share aside for him to pick up when he gets out of jail!'

'It was a clever idea of Roddy's, smuggling the plan out by way of those little . . . '

But the wind blew away the rest of what Simmy was saying. Straining their ears, the Five just managed to catch a few more words of the conversation. This time it was the man called Leo speaking.

'Nine tomorrow night, at the Pink House, and then we'll . . . '

The two men had started to walk on. The Five couldn't follow them across the waste ground without the risk of being seen, so they had to let them go.

It was beginning to get dark, and they decided to go home to Kirrin Cottage, where they could sit in the warm and discuss the results of their after-noon's expedition.

They all gathered in the boys' room to talk over the information they had picked up. George started.

'Well – so now we're sure that one of the thieves is Simeon Ruddock, Simmy for short. But it sounds as if his boss is the other man – the one whose first name is Leo.'

'Unless it's this man called Roddy they were talking about,' said Julian. 'We know *he's* involved in some way!'

'And we know he's in prison too,' added Anne.

'So those are the few facts we're sure of,' said Dick. 'Now we have to fit them together with the conversation we heard. Leo was rather angry with Simmy for leaving somewhere before a delivery of something. Leaving where? And a delivery of what?'

George thought, frowning slightly. 'I think I know!' she said at last. 'Leo went on to talk about a "risky operation" and then a "break-in". He probably meant the theft of Jean's Christmas tree was the risky operation – and as for the break-in, that was obviously the burglary at the Kirrin Stores!'

'And of course the delivery they were talking about was the delivery of the teddy bears!' cried Anne excitedly. 'We know they arrived late – Bob told us so! And only the teddy bears were stolen!'

'Yes,' said Julian. 'That all sounds logical, George. Simmy must have had a temporary job working at the Kirrin Stores when they were extra busy before Christmas. So he'd have expected to be able to look for the plan hidden in one of the teddy bears when they arrived at the shop. But as they came late, after his job had finished, the thieves had to get hold, first, of the bears decorating the Thompsons' Christmas tree, and then, when it wasn't in any of those, they had to steal the bears left in the shop!'

'And as luck would have it, none of them was the right bear!' said George. 'The plan was inside the one Julian bought for Anne! Well, now we know for sure that it *is* a plan, and it must show how to find what Simmy called "the goods". But what did he mean by *that*?'

'We can't know for sure,' said Dick. 'But he did seem to be talking about something very valuable, if they're planning to smuggle it out of the country and sell it abroad. And he sounded sure it would be very profitable!'

'And don't forget, there'll be a share of the profits put aside for their accomplice Roddy,' Julian reminded the others.

'If you ask me,' said George, 'he's not just an accomplice, he's the leader of the gang, even if he's in prison at the moment! He sounds like the master-mind to me! I'm sure *he* drew up the plan, and he had the clever idea of getting it to the others by means of – '

'The little teddy bears!' cried Anne.

'Yes,' agreed George. 'Though I'm still bothered about one thing. If Roddy's in prison, how would he manage to have a bear mascot with him, and get it sent out with a whole lot of other bears just like it, to a place where he'd know his friends could pick it up?'

'I know!' cried Dick, suddenly clapping his forehead. 'I've had an absolute brainwave!'

'Modest as ever!' grinned his brother.

'Well, I *have*! Listen! Prisoners work while they're in jail – sewing mailbags and so on, don't they? Well, why shouldn't they have been making little soft toys for sale too? I bet you that's the explanation. Roddy would only have had to hide his plan in the stuffing of one of the toys he was making. He probably found out somehow what shop had ordered that batch of bears, and put his friends on the right trail to get them!'

'Yes – that *is* a clever idea, Dick,' cried George. 'I'm sure you've guessed right. But after all, that doesn't really matter – never mind *how* they did it, they *did* do it! The thing now is to stop the men from getting hold of the "goods" they're after, whatever those are. Well, we know that Simmy and Leo are to meet at a place called the Pink House tomorrow night. Perhaps that's where the goods are! We must find out where this Pink House is, and be there at the same time as Simmy and Leo!'

'There's nothing to prove it's anywhere near here,' Julian pointed out. 'Still, I suppose we'd better assume and hope it is, and act accordingly. They've picked a good time to meet, haven't they? It's New Year's Eve tomorrow, and at nine o'clock in the evening there won't be many people out and about in the countryside. Everyone will be either at home or at a party, waiting to see the New Year in!'

'Except for us!' said George. 'Supper at home will be later than usual, I expect – but by nine o'clock we can easily say we want to go and play Scrabble or cards by ourselves in the games room.'

'Yes,' said Dick, 'and then we can seize our opportunity to go out! Uncle Quentin and Aunt Fanny won't know we've gone at all – I hope!'

'First we have to find out where the Pink House is,' Anne reminded them.

'Well, we've still got most of tomorrow to do that,' said George.

'We've been lucky so far – let's just hope our luck holds! It *can't* let us down now, can it, Timmy?'

'Woof!' Timmy assured his mistress.

Chapter Nine

THE PINK HOUSE

The children went back to Middleton early next morning. There was an icy cold wind blowing, and the bicycle ride wasn't much fun – and when they got there, the children realised they weren't sure just *how* to make inquiries without awakening suspicion. Suppose Simmy himself got wind of what they were doing? They certainly didn't want that.

But Julian soon thought of a good idea.

'Let's go into the *other* café!' he said, pointing to the Grand Café's competitor. It was called The Black Cat. 'We can buy ourselves some nice hot cocoa there to warm us up, and ask questions at the same time.'

So the children found a table in The Black Cat café. They sat down and looked round. There weren't many people in the place at this time in the morning. A fair-haired boy was acting as waiter. He had an honest, smiling face and he looked rather nice. The children heard someone call him Peter, and from what was said they gathered that he was the son of the café proprietor.

When Peter came over to take their order, he patted Timmy's head.

'I say – that's a fine dog you've got!' he said, with a smile.

Timmy looked pleased, and George beamed.

'Yes, he is!' she agreed. 'And he's brave and intelligent too. Of course, he isn't exactly a drawing-room sort of dog!'

'No, I can see that!' said the boy, with another smile. 'I can't imagine *him* sitting on someone's lap with a pink bow round his neck!'

George suddenly had a brainwave! 'No,' she said, 'although I *did* once tie a pink ribbon round his neck when we were playing about, and he seemed quite pleased with it! He did look funny, though! Do you remember, Anne? It *was* a pink ribbon, wasn't it? Pink, like the Pink House?'

It was a long shot – but to her delight she saw Peter react.

'Goodness, do you know the Pink House?' he said, sounding surprised. 'You're not from these parts, are you? I didn't think I'd ever seen you here before.'

Dick thought it would be a good idea to tell part

82

of the truth at this point.

'No, you haven't!' he said, laughing. 'We came here for the first time yesterday, and that's when we heard someone talking about the Pink House. My cousin's rather fascinated by the idea, that's all. After all, there aren't so many pink houses about! But we don't really know much about it.'

'Oh, it's quite a big, grand place,' said Peter. 'It's an old house, and it's painted pink outside – that's how it gets its name, of course. But it wasn't really famous around here until the arrest of its owner, Roddy Gordon!'

The children exchanged triumphant glances. They could feel their hearts beating faster – they felt sure they were getting somewhere now!

When Peter came back with mugs of steaming cocoa and new, squishy currant buns, George got the conversation going again.

'What was this man Gordon arrested for?' she asked.

'It's quite an interesting story – you mean you've never heard about it? About the stolen paintings?'

The children shook their heads.

'Well,' Peter went on, 'a year ago Gordon was found guilty of stealing some valuable pictures from a London art gallery, and sentenced to four years in prison. But the pictures themselves were never recovered, and he always denied stealing them. There's been no one living in his house since he was arrested.'

'Where exactly is the house?' Anne asked – it seemed the right moment for that question.

Peter told her. Apparently the Pink House stood on a minor road between Middleton and Kirrin. This was just what the children had hoped to find out. Luck was certainly on their side today!

They finished their cocoa, said goodbye to Peter, and then left the café.

'We've still got plenty of time to do some exploring before dinner,' said George. 'And if we can find the house now we won't have to come back this afternoon. I think the fewer people see us in Middleton now the better. I wouldn't like to come face to face with Leo or Simmy here in the High Street!'

On their way, Anne asked the others, 'Do you think this man Roddy Gordon hid the stolen paintings somewhere in his house, then? Before he was arrested, I mean. And they're the "goods" Leo and Simmy were talking about?'

'I should think so,' said Dick. 'Of course the police will have searched the place, and he'd have expected that – so he must have hidden them well. But it looks as if he didn't have time to tell his accomplices exactly *where* he hid them. However, he obviously found some way of getting in touch with them after he was put in prison – and then he smuggled out the plan inside your bear, Anne.'

'And when he comes out of prison, of course,' added Julian, 'he'll be planning to pocket *his* share of the money from the sale of the paintings, and live in luxury on his ill-gotten gains!'

'Only we're not going to let him get away with it,' said George.

Timmy backed her up. 'Woof!'

'Just listen to Timmy!' said Dick, laughing. 'He's saying that Gordon can wave goodbye to that money – *he* won't be getting his hands on any of it!'

'We mustn't be over-confident,' said Julian. 'When a prisoner behaves well in jail, he often gets a remission of his sentence for good conduct, doesn't he? It may not be long before Gordon's on the loose again!'

'Well, never mind that now – look, here's the Pink House!' said George.

The Five stopped – even Timmy looked at the house with interest. There was no mistaking it. It was a *very* pink house! The building was an old Elizabethan half-timbered one, and the plaster in between the dark old beams was painted bright pink. The wooden shutters were pink too. The roof of the house was thatched, and there were some steps up to the front door. The Pink House stood all alone, far from any other buildings, in the middle of a garden which had run wild.

The Pink House stood in a garden which had run wild.

The Five rode off into the night, pedalling as hard as they could.

'Let's explore!' suggested Dick.'There doesn't seem to be anyone around. It's now or never if we want to find our way about – and that could come in very useful this evening.'

George pushed the garden gate. It was rusty and squealed on its hinges as it opened – but it did open.

'Oh, good!' she said. 'It's not locked.'

The children hid their bicycles in the ditch beside the road, and then, going in single file, they walked down the gravel path towards the house. Timmy trotted along in front, nose in the air, ready to warn the children if he picked up any suspicious scent.

But unlike the garden gate, the doors of the house itself were locked.

'No luck,' said Dick, after trying all the doors and then the shuttered windows. 'It's well and truly locked up. Oh, bother ! We can't get in.'

'That may be just as well,' Julian pointed out. 'It wouldn't look very good if we were found here breaking and entering!'

George didn't say anything. She was busy examining two ventilator grilles at ground level. They were like long, narrow windows without any glass, but with bars over them, and it looked as if they were meant to let air and a bit of light into the cellar of the Pink House.

'I feel sure the paintings are hidden down there

in the cellar!' she told the others. 'Oh, if only we had a chance to explore! I'm sure we could find them with the help of Gordon's plan!'

But there was nothing the Five coud do just now, so they went home to Kirrin Cottage. Oh, how impatient they felt! It seemed as if that evening would never come. And when it did, would they manage to slip out of the house without being noticed by Uncle Quentin and Aunt Fanny? If they couldn't do that, all their fine plans would come to nothing.

Uncle Quentin and Aunt Fanny had asked a married couple who were friends of theirs to come and see the New Year in with them at Kirrin Cottage. After supper there was still a long time to wait until midnight, so the four grown-ups decided to go into the sitting room and play bridge.

'And once they've started their game, I'm sure they won't come out of the sitting room till it's very nearly midnight!' George gleefully told her cousins. 'So we're free to do whatever we like. It'll be easy to go out!'

'Suppose someone notices we've gone, though?' said Anne, sounding a little worried.

'That's just a risk we'll have to take – so come on, Anne! We're off!'

The four cousins went to fetch their bicycles. George had strapped the biggest bicycle basket they had on hers, so that Timmy could have a ride for once and wouldn't have to run through the mud. He got into the basket and sat there, looking very pleased. Then they all rode off into the night.

They pedalled as hard as they could – but would they get there in time? It was all very well for George and Dick to sound full of confidence, but they couldn't be sure what they would find waiting for them at their journey's end. And as for Julian and Anne, who were more cautious and sensible by nature, *they* were both thinking that none of them were certain of anything. All their theories about tonight were based on a few scraps of conversation they'd overheard. Mightn't they have been building castles in the air?

'I wonder if Simmy and his accomplice really are planning to meet at the Pink House?' Anne was saying to herself.

And Julian was worrying too, as *he* wondered if the piece of paper really showed where the paintings were hidden. It could be about something quite different!

Now and then George patted her pocket, to make sure the original plan was still there. She had snatched it up at the last minute. She was so glad to think that the enemy only had a useless imitation!

Just before they reached the Pink House, the Five left their bicycles by the roadside, and walked on. Taking plenty of precautions, they approached Roddy Gordon's house – and they saw immediately that they had been right! The garden gate was standing open, and a faint light filtered out through one of the ventilator grilles at the end of the gravel path.

'You see?' whispered George triumphantly. 'I *was* right after all!'

Chapter Ten

IN THE CELLAR

The children and Timmy, shadowy figures in the dark, made their way over to the ventilator grille and bent down to peer in. There was enough space between the bars for them to have quite a good view, and it was a remarkable sight they saw down in the cellar of the Pink House. Simmy and his accomplice were there. The cellar had a mud floor, and Simmy was busy digging up the west corner of it, while Leo gave him instructions. Leo was looking at the plan he was holding – the plan that Julian had traced. There was a third person there too, holding a big hurricane lamp to give them enough light to see by. The children guessed that the electricity in the house must have been cut off when Roddy Gordon went to prison.

Anne craned her neck. 'Oh!' she whispered.

'I've seen that woman before. She's the one who wanted me to give her Blue Bear!'

Anne was quite right. When she pointed it out, George, Julian and Dick recognised the woman too. They remembered talking to her in Kirrin two days after Christmas.

Simmy was hard at work with a pickaxe. Chunks of earth flew up from the cellar floor!

'It must be there – it *must*!' Leo kept saying, looking at the plan. 'Carry on, Simmy – keep going!'

After a while Simmy stopped to mop his face. It was running with sweat.

'Why don't *you* have a go, Leo?' he grumbled. 'This floor's hard as concrete!'

'Okay – move over and I'll take a turn. Let's have some more light over here, Irene.'

The woman put her hurricane lamp down on the floor and lit a second lantern. Leo had already taken over the pickaxe and was going on with the work. Soon the two men, taking turns and changing over at regular intervals, had dug up the whole of that corner of the cellar.

Above them, looking down through the ventilator grille, the children were so fascinated that they didn't even notice the cold night air! And when Simmy threw his pickaxe down in disgust they could hardly help laughing.

'Not a trace of it! I give up!' said the young man.

'Roddy marked the place where the trunk's hidden so carefully on the plan – but we haven't found anything.'

'We'll just have to dig deeper,' said Leo. 'It does look as if the plan says we'll find it one foot down – but Roddy's put a sort of flourish at the top of his figure 1, and I suppose it might be a 7 instead.'

'You mean we've got to dig *seven feet* down?' said Simmy, horrified. 'Why on earth would he have buried the canvases so deep. That's crazy!'

'You'd better try, all the same,' said the woman called Irene. 'After all, we've got plenty of time!'

'It's all right for *you* to talk!' Leo told her. 'You're not doing the digging!'

'There are two pickaxes, aren't there? Why don't you both dig at once?'

'And risk hitting each other by mistake? Move over, Simmy. I'll take another turn.'

George straightened up, signing to her cousins to follow her, and they all retreated from the ventilator grille in silence.

'We can't stay there for ever getting frozen!' George whispered. 'Of course the men will never find the paintings Roddy Gordon buried, since they're using the back-to-front plan! I think what we'd better do is wait for them to come out of the house. And when they've given up and gone away, *we* can try to get in and look for the paintings ourselves!'

'All right,' said Dick. 'But where can we wait without freezing to death?'

'In the thieves' car!' said George boldly. 'Look — that must be it standing among the trees there, near the garden gate. If they've left it unlocked . . .'

And they had! The car doors were open. The children and Timmy got in, glad to be out of the cold wind and thinking what a good trick this was to play on the thieves!

'Why don't you three try to get a little sleep?' said Julian. 'I'll keep watch.'

Dick, George and Anne were just dozing off when Julian shook them.

'Quick — we must get out! They're coming back.'

In a flash, the children slipped out of the car and hid among the trees. They could see Simmy and his two friends coming. The three of them didn't look at all pleased, and they were arguing hotly.

'Gordon was just having us on!' said Simmy.

'No, that's impossible — why would he want to?' objected Leo. 'We'll come back again tomorrow evening, and dig up the whole of that cellar if we have to!'

'I'm freezing!' grumbled Irene.

They got into their car, started it up, and drove off.

'Oh, good!' said George. 'Did you notice — they didn't bring their tools with them! That means the tools are still in the house, and they'll make things easier for us!'

'Go easy, George,' said Julian. 'How are we going to get into the house ourselves? That's the first problem!'

'Oh, we'll find a way!' said Dick cheerfully.

But although the children tried all the doors and windows, it was no good. They couldn't find any way at all to get in. As for the ventilator grilles, they had strong bars over them, and there wasn't nearly enough space between the bars for anyone to slip through.

'Oh, blow!' said Dick crossly. 'I give up!'

At that very moment, Anne saw something shiny in the moonlight, lying on the gravel of the garden path. She bent down to pick it up. It was a key!

'I say!' cried Dick. 'Just suppose it's the front door key!'

He ran up the steps to the house, put the key into the lock, turned it — and the door opened! In a moment the children were inside the Pink House!

'That'll teach them to quarrel!' said Anne. 'If they hadn't been so busy being nasty to each other they'd have noticed dropping the key!'

'Come on, quick!' said George. 'Let's get down to the cellar!'

Once they were down there, Anne lit the two hurricane lamps again. Her brothers found both pickaxes, and George unfolded their plan – the real one! A couple of minutes later, the boys were busy digging away in the *east* corner of the cellar, at the spot shown on Gordon's sketch. The ground there turned out to be quite crumbly and easy to dig. When Dick got tired George took over and helped Julian. As she worked, she muttered, 'We should find it a foot down . . . keep going, Ju!'

At last, Julian's pickaxe struck something hard with a metallic sound. The children dug harder than ever, and soon they uncovered a tin trunk.

Imagine their feelings when they lifted its lid!

All they could see at first were some coloured rolls of canvas carefully packed side by side. George took one out and unrolled it.

'Gosh!' said Julian, whistling. 'I know what *that* is! It's a very famous modern painting called "Woman with Water-lilies!" I saw a reproduction of it in the newspaper when it was stolen.'

'We've done it!' cried Dick. 'Here are the missing paintings all right! Now all we have to do is get them safely back to Kirrin Cottage, and Uncle Quentin can hand them over to the police.'

'The trunk's too heavy for us to carry it all the way back to Kirrin Cottage, even if we weren't on our bikes,' Julian pointed out. 'I think the best thing to do is hide it in the garden, buried under a heap of dead leaves perhaps, and then go to the nearest police station!'

George was smiling happily. 'I wonder what our

friends Simmy and Leo would say if they could see us now?' she said.

'We'd say thank you very much, young man!' a familiar voice unexpectedly replied. 'I see you've done the job for us! I really must congratulate myself for losing that front door key. I was coming back to look for it when I happened to see a light in the cellar – you were all so busy you didn't even hear us coming!'

It was Leo! Of course, he still thought George was a boy. She turned to look at him in horror. Simmy was there too, laughing. Julian, Dick and Anne felt just as shocked as George. At the very moment when they thought they'd succeeded, the thieves had turned the tables on them!

Suddenly something occurred to George. Why hadn't Timmy barked, to warn them. She looked round in panic. Timmy wasn't in the cellar at all!

'My dog!' she cried. 'What have you done with my dog?'

Leo laughed.

'Unlike you, my lad, your dog *did* hear us coming. He tried to attack us too, but we were too quick for him. I managed to knock him out as he was going for my friend's throat.'

'You've probably killed him!' wailed George. And she leaped at Leo like a wild-cat. But Simmy grabbed her. Julian and Dick were coming to their cousin's aid, but Leo stopped them by saying in a

'There - nicely trussed like Christmas turkeys,' said Leo.

threatening voice, 'None of that! Move another inch and I'll get Simmy there to wring your young friend's neck.'

Then everything happened very fast. There were some pieces of washing line lying about the cellar, and with Simmy's help Leo used them to tie the children up.

'There — nicely trussed like Christmas turkeys!' he said. 'That'll teach you to go playing detectives — though I must admit you tricked us nicely, handing us a plan traced the wrong way round! Do you know, I was beginning to have my doubts about that plan! Well — now all we have to do is go off with the goods and wish you a Happy New Year! Ha, ha, ha! By the time you're found — and goodness knows just when *that* will be — it certainly *will* be the New Year, and we'll be well away! As a matter of fact you're doing us a good turn by forcing us to leave the country now. We'll have to keep Gordon's share of the loot for ourselves — we can't wait about for him to come out of prison! I don't suppose he'll be very pleased, but that's just too bad! Come on, Simmy, and don't forget the lamps!'

A moment later the cellar door slammed shut behind the thieves — and the valuable paintings!

Chapter Eleven

TIMMY TO THE RESCUE!

George was furious. She was badly worried about poor Timmy, and she couldn't forgive herself for letting the men take them by surprise.

'We simply *must* get· out of here!' she cried, struggling to loosen the cords tying her.

'They didn't gag us,' Julian pointed out. 'I suppose that means that even if we do shout no one will hear us from the road, and they know it!'

'And they took the light away!' said Anne, in a scared little voice. 'There's nothing but the moonlight to show us anything.'

'I'm going to try rubbing the rope tying me against the wall here,' said Julian. 'I might be able to wear it through like that.'

But hard as he tried, he got nowhere. Then, suddenly, George pricked up her ears. She thought she heard a whimpering noise on the stairs down to the cellar.

'That's Timmy!' she cried in relief. 'He isn't dead after all! Oh, Timmy – poor, dear old Timmy!'

Then she heard another noise – a cheering one! It was the sound of the cellar door squealing on its hinges as it swung open.

'Oh, good!' said Dick. 'Simmy and Leo slammed that door so hard behind them that it didn't close properly, and now it's opened again!'

'Timmy! Timmy!' called George.

Soon she felt her dog's nose against her cheek, and then his rough tongue was licking her face all over.

'Timmy – oh, what a licky dog you are!' she cried. 'Now, Timmy – help me, please!'

Timmy was a very intelligent dog, but even he couldn't find a way to free his mistress directly. First he tried dragging her out of the cellar by her clothes, but of course that was no good – she was too heavy for him. Then, with George urging him on, he started chewing through the rope binding her hands. It was hard work! Sometimes he got discouraged and went back to licking George's face, and she had to speak sternly to him to make him go back to chewing instead. But at long last he had chewed right through the rope, and it gave way.

George uttered an exclamation of triumph.

'My hands are free,' she told the others. 'But they feel terribly numb. Just give me a moment to rub some life into them, and then I'll untie you too. Oh, Timmy, whatever would we do without you?'

George didn't waste time trying to untie the rope round her ankles – she just rolled across the floor until she could reach Julian, and, putting her hand in her cousin's pocket, she took out the penknife he always carried with him. In a moment she had set herself free and cut the ropes round the other children too.

Anne, feeling very upset, was crying quietly.

'Stop crying, you baby!' said George gruffly. 'The danger's over now – but we must act fast if we want to get the thieves arrested and recover the paintings! Come on – let's go!'

They all hurried out of the cellar which had been the scene of such excitement. The thieves had locked the front door again, but it wasn't difficult to open the window shutters from inside, so the children managed to get out of one of the ground floor windows.

'Now we must get to the police station as fast as we can,' said Dick.

'Hold on a minute,' said Julian. 'We don't know if there *is* a police station at Middleton – it's not a very big place. *I* think we'd better go straight to Kirrin police station. They know us there, and we're almost halfway to Kirrin already on this road.'

'Yes,' agreed George. 'That would save time in case we don't find any police in Middleton. We can just go straight on along the road!'

But that was easier said than done. It was a very cold night, and the moon had disappeared behind thick clouds now, so it was very dark too. The children had been bicycling along for rather a long time when they began to feel worried.

'That's funny!' said Anne. 'I'd have thought we ought to be near Kirrin now.'

'I hope we aren't lost,' said Dick anxiously.

'Wait a minute – I can see a sign-board,' said George.

They got off their bicycles to look – but whatever the board had once said, it had been washed away by years of rain, and the children were none the wiser.

'I'm afraid we must have gone over a crossroads without noticing,' said Julian gloomily. 'The best thing would be to go back!'

But at that moment two beams of light suddenly pierced the darkness, and with a squeal of brakes, a car stopped beside the children.

It was a police patrol car, with an inspector and a sergeant inside it! They were out and about on New Year's Eve to keep an eye on empty houses and watch for speeding drivers, or people who

Two beams of light suddenly pierced the darkness.

'What are you doing out here?' asked the Inspector.

might get rowdy after a party. They certainly hadn't expected to come across four children and a dog, looking lost!

Of course, George knew they would not have been lost for long. They'd probably only gone a little out of their way, and she was sure she could always count on Timmy's nose to get them home again. However, she was quite relieved to see the police car stop. 'Good!' she thought. 'They can tell us the way back to Kirrin.'

But she didn't have time to ask, because the two policemen were getting out of the car, and the Inspector was speaking rather sternly to the children.

'Well, children — what do you think you're doing out at this time of night, in the middle of the country?'

Timmy didn't like the Inspector's tone of voice. He began growling.

'Keep that dog of yours under control!' added the policman. 'He looks vicious!'

George protested indignantly. But as it happened, the Inspector was in a bad temper. He wished he wasn't on duty that night. He'd far rather have been at home seeing the New Year in with his wife and family. Like so many other people, he thought George was a boy, and her attitude annoyed him.

'Pretty ready with your tongue, aren't you, my

lad?' he said. 'But you haven't answered my question. What are you doing out here?'

'We're on our way to Kirrin,' Julian told him.

'That's a likely story! Why, you're going in exactly the wrong direction!'

'Oh dear – I was afraid of that,' Julian admitted. 'We've lost our way, that's all.'

'Huh! And where did you come from?'

'Kirrin,' Anne explained.

'Now don't you play games with me, young lady! You can't both have come from Kirrin *and* be going there! People don't go for bicycle rides for pleasure on a cold New Year's Eve!'

'The fact is we've been visiting Middleton, and now we're on our way back to Kirrin,' Dick told the Inspector.

'It all sounds a bit fishy to me. In my opinion you're running away from home!'

'Unless they're tramps or gypsies up to no good,' suggested the Sergeant. 'Just look at 'em, sir! Their clothes are all torn and dirty.'

An evening spent down in a cellar had certainly not done the children's jeans and anoraks any good! And they had been lying on the dusty floor when they were tied up, too.

'Look – it's nothing like you think!' Dick began.

'These bicycles they're riding look quite new as well,' the Inspector said, interrupting him rudely. 'Pinched them from somewhere, did you?'

'Now wait a minute!' said Julian indignantly. 'We're perfectly honest! In fact we were on our way to Kirrin police station to make a statement!'

'Well, well, well!' said the Sergeant, sarcastically. 'And just what were you going to make a statement about, may I ask?'

George went boldly up to him and said, in a rather dramatic voice, 'We wanted to tell the police we'd found the valuable paintings stolen by Roddy Gordon a year ago, and we were going to tell them how to arrest his accomplices too!'

'Oh, was *that* all, eh?' said the sergeant, roaring with laughter. 'You've certainly got a cheek, young fellow! You think the police would swallow a tale like that?'

'But it's *true*!' cried Anne, near tears.

'It's far too cold to stand here arguing,' the Inspector interrupted. 'You can leave the bikes here and we'll pick them up later. Now, hop into our car. We're going on to Pendle St John. We'll take you to the police station there, and check your identity. We'll check as much as we can of what you've said, too. It may take a bit of time, but I can assure you it'll all be done according to the rules!'

He was interrupted by an indignant cry from Dick. 'But if you keep us some time at the police station, it may be too late!' Dick said. 'The thieves will have gone goodness only knows where – taking the paintings with them! And you'll never get them then!'

'You've got no right to stop us, when we're doing our best to help the police!' added George.

'I say – just listen to the lad,' said the Inspector, laughing. 'Who d'you think you are, eh? Sherlock Holmes?'

'I am not a lad!' said George stiffly. Just for once she felt like saying so, because the Inspector was annoying her so much that she wanted to contradict him! 'I'm a girl, and my name is Georgina Kirrin, daughter of Quentin Kirrin the famous scientist, and – '

'Now just get into the car,' said the Sergeant.

The children tried to resist when the police officers made them get into the car, but it was no good.

'I've had quite enough of all this!' said the Inspector. 'Now then – off we go!'

George was unusually quiet during the short drive – but she wasn't wasting any time. She had furtively taken a handkerchief out of her pocket, and using a ballpoint pen she managed to scribble a short message to her father on it. Then she tied the handkerchief to Timmy's collar. The Inspector and the Sergeant, sitting in the front of the car, hadn't noticed anything.

When the car stopped outside Pendle St John police station, George let her cousins get out first.

As she was following them, she leaned down to Timmy and told him, under her breath, 'Home, Timmy! Go on, quick! Home!' Then she gave him a little tap and repeated, 'Home – good dog! Go!'

That was all Timmy needed. He looked at her, and realising that she really did want him to leave her, he wagged his tail and vanished into the night. It all happened so fast that the two police officers didn't realise he was gone until they were all inside the police station.

'Hallo, that dog's made off!' said the Inspector.

'Never mind,' said the Sergeant. 'Come along, kids!'

Chapter Twelve

AT THE POLICE STATION

There were only two policemen on duty in Pendle St John police station – a sergeant and a constable. The two police officers from the patrol car handed the children over to them.

'We're more or less sure these kids have run away from home,' they told the Pendle St John police. 'We found them cycling along the road, going the opposite way from where they said they were bound, and telling some most unlikely stories!'

Julian bristled with annoyance. 'We have *not* run away from home!' he protested. 'Or anywhere else!'

'We'll see about that when we get in touch with your parents! Meanwhile you'll just have to wait while we write our reports.'

While the four men were filling in forms, George

and her cousins, sitting side by side on a bench, exchanged despairing glances.

'Where's Timmy?' whispered Anne.

'On his way back to Kirrin Cottage!' said George. 'I just hope he doesn't lose my hanky on the way – I scribbled an SOS message on it. It must be quite late by now . . . '

'Yes – it's nearly midnight,' Dick told her, looking at his watch. 'Golly – what will Uncle Quentin say to us? Still, you were quite right to try and get a message to him, George. This is urgent!'

The policemen came over and began to ask the children questions. It was Julian who suggested that they could telephone Kirrin Cottage, but when they tried it was no good. The line was dead! Probably a tree had blown down across the wire, or something like that, and it certainly wouldn't be put right until after New Year's Day.

The children were on tenterhooks. Every extra minute that went by made it easier for the thieves to get away, and less likely that they would ever be captured.

A church clock somewhere in the distance had struck one by the time they heard a car stop outside the police station. Then there came the sound of a firm and rather indignant voice.

'It's my father!' George whispered.

A moment later Uncle Quentin appeared, followed by Timmy. He had told the policemen who he was, and said he would be responsible for the children – who were all looking rather downcast. George was biting her lip with annoyance.

After talking to the policemen for a while, her father turned to her. He was looking rather severe. In the background, the officers from the police car were watching and seemed rather surprised to find the children had been telling the truth about who they were – while the Pendle St John policemen were looking amused!

'Well,' said Uncle Quentin, in a cutting voice. 'What's all this? I thought you four were quietly playing games at home – and all the time you were out and about, getting yourselves picked up by the police! If Timmy hadn't come whining at the door . . . well, would you be good enough to tell me what all this *is* about, George?'

Given a chance to explain, George took it! It was just too bad if her father was going to punish her later – the main thing now was to get the thieves caught and recover the stolen paintings!

'Well, Father, we've been trying to solve another mystery, and we did it too!' she said. 'I'll tell you about it as fast as I can – this is what happened!'

And with the others joining in from time to time, George told the story of their amazing Christmas adventures. The policemen were astonished.

'But this is incredible!' said the Inspector from the police car. 'These kids are letting their imagination run away with them!'

'I don't think so,' Uncle Quentin told him. 'They have quite a gift for getting mixed up in trouble, but they're not liars. We had better believe what they say and act on their information as fast as possible! And I'm quite sure that if anything comes of all this, you, gentlemen, will get full credit for it!'

That worked like a charm — suddenly the policemen were in a great hurry! The Pendle St John police got on the telephone, and the two officers from the patrol car went back to it, to send messages on their radio. A few minutes later the Inspector came back.

'There'll be reinforcements coming soon,' he said. 'Meanwhile, we'd better get moving ourselves!'

He turned to Uncle Quentin and the Five, and said, 'Maybe one of these kids can show me where Simeon Ruddock lives? He's the only one of the suspects whose full name we know, and if he's at home we can get him to tell us where to pick the others up.'

'If the three of them aren't all some way off by now,' said the Sergeant gloomily.

'Well, we must still try! What about it, children?'

'We don't actually know Simmy's address,' said George, 'but I should think anyone in Middleton could tell you. It's not a very big place. Can we come with you?

The Inspector started to say no, but in the end George managed to convince him that it might be useful to have them on the spot, since they knew the suspects by sight, and he agreed.

'We'll all follow you in my car,' Uncle Quentin decided, much to the children's delight.

The Inspector and Sergeant were sending another radio message back to their headquarters. They explained that they were going to Middleton and would keep in touch with Pendle St John police station, where the reinforcements would soon arrive. Then they started off, followed by Uncle Quentin in his own car, with the children and Timmy sitting inside.

The Black Cat café was all lit up with Japanese lanterns for the New Year celebrations. The two cars stopped outside it, and George and her cousins hurried over to the policemen.

'I say – we know Peter, the son of the café proprietor here,' said Dick. 'If you like, I could go in on my own and ask him where Simmy lives. No one will take much notice of me.'

'All right,' said the Inspector. 'Yes – that's a good idea. We don't want people to see us about and realise we're after young Ruddock. Someone might warn him!'

Dick slipped into the café. It was very full

tonight, with people who had been seeing the New Year in. But Dick managed to stop Peter as he ran busily from table to table.

'Hey – Peter! Remember me?' he said. 'Listen, I want to ask you something. Where exactly does Simmy Ruddock live?'

'Simmy Ruddock? You're not a friend of *his*, are you? I warn you, he's no good!'

'No, I'm not a friend of his, but I want to get in touch with him.'

'Well, go down the High Street to the Grand Café, and then turn first left,' said Peter. 'Keep on to the end of the road, and it's the very last house. It belongs to Simmy's brother Joe.'

'Thanks, old chap – I'm very grateful!'

Dick passed on the information to the policemen, and they all got back into the two cars again. But when they got to the house Peter had described, they were disappointed to see there was no light in any of the windows. The Sergeant hammered on the door, and after a while a light did show at the landing window. Then the door opened.

A tall, strong young man appeared on the doorstep.

'Hallo – what's up?' he asked, seeing so many shadowy figures moving about. 'Who are you, and what do you want?'

'We're police. Does Simeon Ruddock live here?' asked the Inspector, coming forward.

Dick stopped Peter as he ran busily from table to table.

'Hallo - what's up?' asked the tall young man.

The young man looked downcast. 'So that was it!' he exclaimed. 'I suppose my brother's been up to his tricks again? Yes, he did live here, but –'

'*Did?*'cried George, unable to keep herself from interrupting. 'You mean he's left?'

Joe Ruddock looked at the children, rather surprised, and then nodded.

'Yes, Simmy came to get his things about two hours ago,' he said. 'He told me he'd got a job abroad, and said he had to leave tonight. He sounded as if he was going for good.'

'Leaving tonight!' said the Inspector. 'And I suppose he didn't tell you just *where* he was going in the middle of the New Year holiday?'

'No,' said Joe, 'but I do know where he's leaving *from*! I'm sure he said he was starting out tonight from Kirrin. He was talking a lot, and seemed very pleased about something – in fact he was in such a cheerful mood, that's why I rather suspected he'd been up to no good. What's he gone and done now?'

'I'm afraid we can't tell you yet, but thanks for your help – and I'm sorry about your trouble, sir,' said the Inspector sympathetically. 'Good night!'

Then Uncle Quentin and the police officers held a quick consultation.

'It isn't as if Kirrin was a big port with international ferries leaving from it,' said the Inspector. 'It's only a little fishing village! So if our friend is leaving from Kirrin it means he must be going on board a fishing boat, or even a motor launch. I suspect that in his cheerful mood he let part of the truth out – he and his accomplices *are* leaving the country, planning to sell the stolen pictures abroad and live on the proceeds!'

'And they must be well away by now,' said the Sergeant again, gloomily.

'I'm not so sure,' said Julian. 'The three of them aren't necessarily in a great hurry! *They* think we're still tied up in the cellar of the Pink House, remember, unable to raise the alarm!'

'What's more,' added George, 'the way things turned out tonight must have made a difference in their plans. They hadn't *expected* to be leaving tonight, so Leo and Simmy and Irene probably didn't have everything ready. Even if they had a boat moored off Kirrin, they'll still have needed to stock it up with provisions, and fill the fuel tank and so on!'

'Not bad reasoning, young people!' the Inspector admitted. The children were quite beginning to like him after all! 'Well then, the sooner we get to Kirrin the better!'

Chapter Thirteen

BACK TO KIRRIN

And once again everybody got back into the two cars. They drove fast along the road to Kirrin. As they passed the Pink House, which was just visible in the dark, George pointed to it and told her father, 'That's where we found the stolen paintings – and we'd still be prisoners there, but for dear, brave Timmy!'

When they reached Kirrin the moon had come out from behind the clouds again and was lighting up the little harbour. Fishing boats and motor boats were bobbing about side by side on the water. It all seemed much calmer and quieter now!

'Where do we look first?' said the Sergeant.

Standing on the jetty, Uncle Quentin, the policemen and the children glanced around them – but there was nothing out of the ordinary to be seen.

'We'll walk along the shore,' the Inspector decided. 'Perhaps we may spot something!'

'I'll come with you,' Uncle Quentin told him. 'And as for you children you'd better wait in the car.'

'Oh, Father!' George protested. 'Do let us come too!'

'No! It's no use, George – you must do as I say. I'll be back soon.'

The Inspector sent another radio message to Pendle St John police station to tell them where he was, saying the reinforcements were to join them at Kirrin harbour. Then the three men walked off into the dark.

Inside the car, the Five were quiet for a while, and then Julian sighed. 'What a pity Uncle Quentin wouldn't let us help!' he said.

'Well, we didn't actually *promise* to stay put here, did we?' said George. 'Let's get out and do some searching ourselves!'

'Oh no!' cried Anne. 'We've already been naughty tonight!'

But just then Timmy said, 'Woof! Woof!' He was standing on his hind legs with his nose out of the open car window. George put her hand on the back of his neck, and felt his hair bristling.

'Ssh!' she whispered. 'Timmy's seen or heard something!'

Out on the jetty, in the faint moonlight, a

shadowy figure had just passed by – the figure of a man carrying two petrol cans.

'Looks like Simmy!' whispered Dick. 'And going the opposite way from Uncle Quentin and the policemen, too!'

'We must do something!' said George.

Anne uttered an exclamation of alarm. 'But Uncle Quentin told us to stay here!'

'That's too bad!' said George. 'Anyway, we're not really being disobedient – *I* think Timmy *needs* to get out of this car! So I've got to let him out, haven't I? And if he goes shooting off after somebody once he's out, I think I ought to follow him!'

As she spoke she was opening the car door – and Timmy did shoot off, like a cannonball, making straight for the furtive shadow! He hadn't forgotten the smell of those men in the cellar of the Pink House. One of them had hit him and tied up his little mistress, and Timmy wanted his revenge! George ran off after him.

It had all happened so fast that Julian, Dick and Anne were rooted to the spot for a moment. In a minute they couldn't see Simmy any more, or George's dog either, and George was running along so fast that soon *she* would be out of sight too.

'Look here, I can't let her take such a risk on her own!' Julian said firmly.

Simmy put down the heavy petrol cans and blew on his numb fingers.

'I'm coming with you!' said Dick.

Anne stayed in the car — she and they all knew she wouldn't be any real help. She was scared, but she bravely resigned herself to waiting on her own.

*   *   *

Simmy's petrol cans were beginning to feel very heavy. He put them down on the ground and stopped to get his breath back.

'Still some way before I get to that wretched boat!' he muttered, blowing on his numb fingers. 'And Leo told me to hurry — I'd like to see *him* hurry, carrying these!'

But his train of thought was interrupted by a violent shock! Something struck Simmy hard between the shoulder-blades, and he fell flat on the muddy jetty.

Before he had recovered, strong teeth seized his right shoulder. The young man began to howl.

'Steady on, Timmy!' cried George. 'I'm coming!'

And in a moment she arrived. Simmy and the dog were a struggling, howling heap rolling about on the jetty, and she was just about to try separating them when Julian and Dick arrived.

'Oh, jolly good!' cried George. 'I'm so glad you decided to come too — with four of us here we can overpower him. Let him go, Timmy! It's all right!'

The good dog let go, and Simmy got up looking miserable. He was terrified of Timmy, and offered no resistance when Julian and Dick took his arms.

'Let's take him back to the car,' George decided. 'My father and the policemen will know how to make him talk and say where he was going to meet the others.'

But Julian was worried. 'We've made rather a lot of noise,' he pointed out. 'If Leo and Irene are anywhere near here they may have heard us – in which case they'll be off without waiting for their friend here!'

'All the more reason to hurry,' said George, quickening her pace.

Now it was Dick's turn to think of something. 'You're forgetting that we don't know just where Uncle Quentin and the others are,' he said. 'How shall we find them in the dark?'

But George was never short of good ideas. She had already thought of a way to let her father know what was going on! As soon as they got back to the car she leaned on the horn, and carefully sounded three short notes, three longer notes, and then three short notes again. She waited a few seconds and then repeated her message.

'Oh, well done, George!' said Dick. 'Three short, three long, three short – that's SOS! The distress signal in Morse code! I'm sure Uncle Quentin will hear it and know what it means.'

Julian and Anne felt a little anxious, all the same. Yes, Uncle Quentin was sure to understand – but could he and the police catch Leo and Irene in time? If those two realised that Simmy had been captured, wouldn't they leave him to his fate and run for it?

And now it was Julian's turn to have a good idea!

Chapter Fourteen

A CHASE AT SEA!

'Listen to me, Simmy!' Julian said suddenly. 'If you'll help us to gain time and tell us where to find your accomplices, I'm sure it will be taken into account at your trial!'

'And if you *don't* talk,' added George in a threatening tone, 'I'll set my dog on you again!'

Simmy was not a particularly brave young man. He realised that now he had nothing to lose, and so he agreed to give the children the information they wanted.

'Leo and his wife Irene are waiting for me in a motor boat, in a little creek just past the jetty,' he told them. 'I left them wrapping up the paintings in a waterproof cover. The fuel tank was almost empty, so they sent me to fetch petrol to fill it.'

'Good!' said George. 'That means they're stuck!'

'A motor boat?' said Dick. 'One of the little ones able to moor off Kirrin! You wouldn't have got very far in that!'

'Leo was only planning to go as far as the big port not far down the coast here. He knows somebody there with a bigger boat, who was going to take us across to France or Holland. I – '

'Oh, here's Uncle Quentin!' cried Anne in relief.

Sure enough, Uncle Quentin and the policemen were running up. 'What's going on?' asked George's father. 'Oh – so you left the car without my permission, did you?' Suddenly he saw their prisoner, and added, 'And who's this?'

'It's Simeon Ruddock, Father. Timmy caught him!'

The Inspector and Sergeant began questioning the young man at once. He was surly, but he agreed to lead them to the place where Leo and his wife were supposed to be waiting for him. This time, in the heat of the moment, Uncle Quentin forgot to tell the children to stay put, so the whole party set off together.

And they had not gone far when the reinforcements arrived. A big black car drew up, and six policemen got out. They fell in with the others.

When they had all gone some way in silence Simmy stopped. 'There they are!' he said, pointing to a motor launch. It was a white boat, so it stood out against the dark sea.

127

Just then the engine of the boat started up. It roared loudly and then the launch set out for the open sea. Leo and Irene must have seen the policemen. They were leaving Simmy in the lurch, staking everything on what little fuel was left in the petrol tank. Their action didn't surprise anyone, but it drew several exclamations of annoyance from the little group.

'We must alert the coastguards!' said the Sergeant.

'That'll take some time – and that precious pair will be well away before the coastguards can do anything,' said the Inspector gloomily.

George had an inspiration. 'Look – there's another motor boat down there, without a tarpaulin or anything over it! We could jump in that and follow them!' she suggested eagerly.

The Inspector didn't hesitate. He jumped in, followed by the Sergeant and Uncle Quentin. The Five followed too.

'You go and raise the alarm at the coastguard station!' the Sergeant shouted to the other policemen still on shore. 'And hurry!'

Much to the children's amusement, it turned out that the Sergeant knew a way to start the motor boat's engine without having its ignition key! Then the Inspector took the wheel. The cold night wind blew in the children's faces, and Timmy's ears streamed out in the breeze. The spray left salt on their faces, but the children didn't mind the weather. Eyes glued to the white blur which was all they could see of Leo and Irene's boat, they had only one thought in their heads — they mustn't lose sight of the enemy!

But the distance between the two boats was growing. Were Leo and Irene going to escape after all?

The mere idea was infuriating! 'Oh, Timmy,' muttered George. 'To think we've been to so much trouble, all for nothing!'

'Don't worry, George,' Anne said sympathetically. 'Remember, they're short of petrol!'

'Nobody would think so, though!' grunted Dick. 'They're setting a tremendous pace!'

'Oh, look!' cried Julian suddenly.

They all strained their eyes — and there, ahead of them, the white blur was getting bigger.

'We're catching up!' said Anne.

'That's not very surprising!' cried George, delighted. 'They've run out of fuel and broken down!'

Sure enough, that was what had happened. The petrol tank of the motor launch had run dry! Now the thieves were at their pursuers' mercy — all the policemen had to do was board the launch and overpower Leo and Irene.

'I hope they don't put up a fight,' muttered Uncle Quentin. He was worried about the

The Five were determined not to lose sight of the enemy.

'You there - surrender!' shouted the Inspector.

children. Turning to them, he told them to go into the little cabin, where they would be out of the way if there was any violence. The four cousins reluctantly obeyed.

When the boat commandeered by the police had almost caught up with the other one, the Inspector cupped his hands round his mouth and called to the villains.

'You there – surrender! You're under arrest! Put your hands up and let us come aboard.'

The thieves might be armed, so there was some danger, but the Inspector and the Sergeant were strong, brave men. As soon as the two motor boats were side by side, they jumped aboard Leo's boat.

Much to Uncle Quentin's relief, Leo and his wife gave in without putting up a fight at all. The Sergeant immediately handcuffed them – they were well and truly caught!

Watching from the cabin of the other boat, the children had seen it all. They hurried out on deck again, feeling full of triumph. But their hopes were dashed when Leo, answering a question put by the Inspector, said in an innocent tone, 'Paintings? I don't know what you mean – there are no paintings on board! We were just going for a boat ride!'

'Oh yes?' said the Inspector. 'And what was that bundle I saw you throw overboard as we came alongside?'

'Bundle? Oh – just some old clothes we wanted to get rid of!'

The two police officers looked at each other in consternation. Had the thieves really thrown their loot into the sea? If so, the valuable paintings were lost, and what was more, there would be no proof against Leo, Simmy and Irene! This was terrible!

'Search the boat if you like!' added Leo sarcastically. 'You won't find anything!'

Well – the Inspector and the Sergeant *did* search the boat. But much to their dismay, they had to face the fact that the paintings were not there. They had disappeared without trace.

George could have wept with fury. 'Oh, please – let *us* have a look too!' she said.

'You children take yourselves seriously, don't you?' muttered the Inspector. But he added, 'All right, if you really want to.'

The Five went on board Leo's motor launch. But they couldn't find anything. There was no sign of the paintings in the little boat.

Then, suddenly, Dick and George looked at each other. Between them, they had been lifting a plastic-covered seat to see what was in the storage space underneath. There was nothing there – but the plastic cover of the seat itself seemed rather over-stuffed!

Anne leaned over it, and saw that it had been slit

open all along one side and rapidly sewn up again.

'Yes – the paintings could be hidden there!' said Julian.

And they were! When the children brought them triumphantly out of the cabin, the Inspector shook hands with them all round and apologised handsomely for being rude to them earlier that night!

'Well done!' he said. 'The bundle we saw thrown overboard was just to deceive us into thinking the paintings were gone! But you found them after all – Sherlock Holmes would have been proud of you!'

*   *   *

New Year's Day was celebrated very happily at Kirrin Cottage. Uncle Quentin wasn't cross with George any more. Quite the opposite – he said he felt very proud of his daughter and her cousins. At twelve noon, the radio newsreader announced the capture of the rest of Roddy Gordon's gang, and said the pictures had been recovered. The Five were mentioned by name.

'Well, well!' said Aunt Fanny, smiling. 'I expect you'll be in all the newspapers tomorrow!'

'Never mind about that,' said Julian. 'We helped the police to get the thieves and the paintings, that's what matters!'

'And we had a good time, as well!' added Dick.

'Yes — that's what we like!' agreed George, smiling. 'Having a good time *and* being useful! Isn't that right, Timmy?'

'Woof!' said Timmy, wagging his tail.

If you have enjoyed this book here are some more adventures that you might like to read, also available from Knight Books:

THE FAMOUS FIVE AND THE MYSTERY OF THE EMERALDS

A summer holiday camping on Kirrin Island is the prospect in store for the Five, and they're eagerly looking forward to exploring the island.

But when George overhears a couple of crooks planning a jewel robbery, the Famous Five set off on a dangerous and thrilling trail.

KNIGHT BOOKS

THE FAMOUS FIVE AND THE MISSING CHEETAH

Arriving for two weeks' stay at Big Hollow, the children are delighted to discover that Tinker has a new friend – a cheetah!

But twenty-four hours later, Attila the cheetah has been kidnapped, and his abductors threaten to shoot him unless they're given the formula for a new, top-secret fuel.

KNIGHT BOOKS

THE FAMOUS FIVE AND THE GOLDEN GALLEON

A wrecked yacht, *The Golden Galleon*, is washed up near Kirrin Island, with a cargo of gold ingots. The Famous Five discover it was used by some bank robbers for their get-away, and when the gold vanishes overnight the Five embark on an exciting treasure hunt.

KNIGHT BOOKS

THE FAMOUS FIVE IN FANCY DRESS

The Five are enjoying a surprise holiday in Scotland when they notice another camper, Rudy, keeps acting most suspiciously. Can he really be involved with a gang of international spies? The Five's attempts to find out, and to foil his plans, soon lead to an unexpected adventure, including dramatic events at a fancy dress party.

KNIGHT BOOKS

MORE EXCITING ADVENTURES FROM KNIGHT BOOKS